Consequences

Carole McKee

DEDICATION

To Trent

Friend, neighbor, co-worker, confidante

You have enriched my life.

Final book of the "Choices" series.

Loraine Carter frowned at the late hour when she heard the doorbell. Who would be visiting at this time of night? It was almost nine-thirty and dark outside. She flipped the switch for the outside light and peered out through the peephole. The auburn-haired woman standing on the stoop of Loraine's suburban ranch home did not look familiar, nor did she look dangerous. Curiosity overtook caution as Loraine pulled the door open.

"Yes?" Loraine's greeting was curt as she eyed the woman warily.

Although she was reasonably attractive, it was easy to see that she must have been through some rough times. Loraine sensed what was close to desperation in this green-eyed woman with faded auburn hair, and pale skin. Dressed in faded worn jeans, and a tee-shirt, covered by a hooded zippered sweatshirt, this woman was no fashion plate. The worn threadbare sneakers on her feet had seen better days, but they were clean. In fact, the entire grizzly ensemble was clean—threadbare but clean. As Loraine waited for the woman to speak, she quickly glanced out to the driveway and spotted the light blue older model Dodge parked halfway between the road and the house.

"I'm looking for Jonathan Riley," the woman finally uttered in a pleasing southern drawl.

"Sorry...there is no one here by that name," Loraine responded, and began to back inside and shut the door.

"Are you Loraine Carter?"

Loraine stopped the door from closing and stared harder at this woman. "Yes, I am. Do I know you?"

"I'm looking for Jonathan."

"There is nobody here by that name."

"But I wrote letters to this address. They weren't returned....so I assumed they had gotten to him."

"But nobody by that name lives here." Loraine was about to tell the woman to leave when she saw the tears glistening in her eyes. It was then that she saw the boy leaning up against the house, his arms folded, staring at the manicured lawn. His dark blonde hair was too long and unkempt, and his clothes on his thin frame were in the same state as the ones the woman wore. There was a sullen attitude surrounding him and there was no mistaking the large chip on his shoulder. Loraine looked away quickly.

"I have a picture. An old one....but maybe.....here....here it is."

She pulled a strip of carnival photo-booth photos from the zippered pouch of her purse and handed them to Loraine. Reluctantly, Loraine took them. Her eyes widened with recognition as she stared at the man in the picture.

"Who are you?" Loraine's voice was ragged as she stared hard into those green eyes. "Where were these pictures taken? And when?"

"My name is Lois Watkins.....and this is my son, Trent. Please...I really need to find Jonathan. Can you help me?"

"How did you know my name?"

"Because...when I sent my letters, I addressed them in care of Loraine Carter."

Somewhere in the recesses of her memory bank, a memory was jogged. Yes, she remembered letters coming here to the house for Jonathan Riley. Oh yeah— she remembered. Holding back a sigh, she backed up and pulled the door open wider.

"Perhaps you should come in and sit down. We should talk."

"Thank you....oh, thank you."

"Come in to the kitchen. Would you like coffee or tea?"

"Oh, I wouldn't mind a cup of tea, but I don't want to put you to any trouble."

"No trouble. I was going to have a cup myself. Trent, would you like a soda? I have a couple in the refrigerator."

The boy nodded, still looking down, but now staring at the thick plush carpeting. Without looking at him, Loraine pulled a soda out of the refrigerator and handed it to him. He silently took it from her.

"Trent....at least thank the lady, for heaven's sake!"

"Trent, would you like to watch a movie? I have several."

Without looking up, the boy nodded and quietly thanked Loraine for the soda. She turned on the television, handed him the remote, and pointed toward the shelf holding a multitude of DVD's. "Pick out any that you might like. Do you know how to work that DVD player?"

Again, the boy nodded and turned toward the shelf. Satisfied that he would be occupied, Loraine returned to the kitchen for tea and truth.

***

Loraine poured the tea and sat down facing Lois. Once again, she quickly assessed the woman and decided that she would be gentle but honest.

"Where and when did you meet him?"

"Jonathan? I met him while I was working. He came into the restaurant for dinner."

"Where and when?"

"In Richmond, Virginia...a little more than sixteen years ago. He gave me his address and told me to write to him....which I did. The letters never came back so I assumed he got them."

Loraine sighed. She couldn't hide the pity she felt for this innocent woman, so her eyes dropped to her teacup. Her mind ran over the events around that time and she realized that her ex-husband must have met this woman on his way to find Lindy, Loraine's foster child. She had run away after Loraine's husband raped her.

"Look.....Lois....there is no Jonathan Riley. The man in the picture is Nelson Sutter, my ex-husband. I'm sorry, but you have been deceived. I don't know everything he told you, but it probably wasn't true."

"I knew you were too young to be his mother. He told me to send the letters in care of Loraine Carter, his mother. He said he was temporarily staying here while his condo was being built."

"His condo is a jail cell."

"He's in jail?"

"Yes...that's what they do to people who rape and kidnap. They incarcerate them."

"W-who did he rape...and kidnap?"

"He raped Lindy, our foster child. She was seventeen and just lovely. Nelson raped her...more than once. She ran away and Nelson was arrested. She left evidence of the rapes. Nelson was released when they couldn't find Lindy to testify. He made it his mission to find her and keep her from talking. He must have been on his way to South Carolina to catch up with her when he met you. What sickens me is....Lindy's last name was Riley."

"So he went to South Carolina and kidnapped her?"

"No...Lindy somehow managed to overpower him. She cut him with some kind of knife, and then a gun went off. Nelson was wounded by the bullet. The authorities brought him back here and he went to prison for fifteen years."

"Then who did he kidnap?"

"Lindy's five-year-old daughter, Samantha."

Lois gasped and stared wide-eyed at Loraine. "Is...is

the child....?"

"The child is fine now. Oddly, Nelson didn't hurt her. He just wanted a big ransom for her so he could leave the country. Somehow he had it in his head that Lindy was to blame for his troubles, and that she should pay."

"So he got caught?"

"Yes, Lindy and her husband Ricky went after him with a vengeance. Luckily for Nelson, the FBI stepped in, or Ricky would have beaten him to death. I can only imagine Ricky's fury. So...once again Nelson was locked up. And that's where he is right now and where he will be for the next twenty years."

Loraine saw the tears glistening in Lois's eyes, and she reached for a box of tissues and set them down in front of her.

"I'm sorry....I don't mean to cry. It's just...it's just that I've had it pretty rough for the past sixteen years. I really needed his help....and now...it doesn't look as though I'll ever get it."

Loraine reached out to pat her hand but retreated when she heard Trent's voice in the doorway.

"So he's in jail. The man is in jail. Nice going, Mom. You yammer at me about making good choices. Did you?"

Loraine watched the boy as he uttered the surly words at his mother, never lifting his eyes from the floor. Reeking of attitude, he moved to the table and dropped onto a chair, jamming his fists into the pockets of his hooded sweatshirt.

"Trent...I had no idea. I'm sorry." Lois turned back to Loraine. "Trent's had a rough time with all of this."

Loraine was puzzled by that statement. *How could this boy have any involvement with...?* She stopped and the realization hit her. Just as she focused on him he raised his eyes up to meet hers; and she knew. Loraine knew, beyond a shadow of a doubt, that she was staring into the golden eyes of Nelson's son.

Chapter 1

It had been a month after Jonathan Riley left Virginia when Lois Watkins realized she was pregnant. At first panic set in, and then the resolve to write to Jonathan. She wouldn't tell him about the baby at first. She would just write a newsy letter and wait for his answer. Maybe she could talk him into coming back to Virginia or maybe he would invite her to Pennsylvania. So she wrote the letter, and waited for an answer. And waited. She wrote again; and again, she waited. No answer.

Although she was resigned to the fact that he was not going to respond, she wrote one more letter after Trent was born. She still did not mention the baby, but she had asked him in the letter to please come visit her. That letter went unanswered, and she never wrote again.

As Lois held baby Trent Riley Watkins in her arms

and rocked him, she was faced with the realization that her one night of pleasure yielded a life of responsibility to this tiny person. She had thrown caution to the wind that night Trent was conceived and now her mother's words came back to haunt her: *"Action without caution is a life with consequences."* And now she understood what her mother meant.

Oh, she loved her baby. She smiled down at his darling little face and breathed in the scent of baby powder. Trent opened his sleepy eyes and stared up in her direction, but his golden eyes had not yet begun to focus on objects yet. *"Yes, my sweet son. I love you. And I promise you that I will take care of you. Some day your daddy may come back...and if he does, he is going to love you as much as I do."* Trent yawned as his eyelids slowly slid down, marking the beginning of his nightly sleep.

Lois laid Trent down in his bed, a blue bassinette surrounded by a blue and white gingham skirt. She removed a blue rattle and set it on the nightstand next to her bed and then she repositioned the brown teddy bear and the blue stuffed dog at the foot of the bassinette so that they were far enough away from the baby. Smiling, she watched him for a moment and then tip-toed back into the small living room to tidy it up. She did the few dishes in the sink and then turned the television on, keeping the sound low. She watched until the news was over and then climbed into bed.

Although she was exhausted, she could not close her eyes. As she lay on her back staring at the ceiling she played her favorite mind game—*What if? What if I'd never met Jonathan? Then I wouldn't have gotten pregnant. What if I hadn't gotten pregnant? I wouldn't have had Trent. What if Jonathan doesn't ever get in touch with me? Then I raise Trent alone. What if he does come back? What if he doesn't want his child? What if he doesn't want to be a part of Trent's life? What if he does? What if he doesn't want me? What if he does?* And this is where the game always stopped and the mind movie began. Her and Jonathan holding each other, laughing. Jonathan looking at his son through adoring eyes. The wedding. Jonathan saying 'I love you'. Oh yeah, it's a box- office-sell-out-tear-jerker. An award-winning chick-flick. Movies of the mind always have happy endings.

Choking back bitter tears, she wrapped her arms around her shoulders and cried into the pillow. "Oh Jonathan...didn't you feel anything when we made love? Was it just sex to you? Why won't you write to me?" She whispered into the pillow in the darkened bedroom. Her heart ached with loneliness and despair, and yes—fears. She was frightened of many things. Raising her son alone, bringing him up right, affording food and housing, and—never, ever having a man hold her again.

She finally fell into a restless sleep and was awakened by Trent's cries at five in the morning. Another day to get through—and many more to come.

Chapter 2

"Why do I have to go to school, Mommy? I don't want to."

"Because it's the law, Trent. Everybody has to go to school."

"But can't you change the law?"

"No, Sweetie, I can't."

"Why not? You can do everything!"

Lois laughed. "Everything but that, Honey. Now let's get going. You're going to love school. There will be books and things to do, and other kids to play with."

"But I'd rather stay home with you, Mommy. Why can't I stay home with you?"

"Because you have to go to school. Besides, mommy is going to look for a job today. I'll pick you up right after school and we can go to the park together. How does that sound?"

"Okay," Trent responded with a sigh.

Smiling down at him, Lois reached for his hand as they started up the sidewalk on the way to the elementary school just a block and a half from their small rented bungalow. Lois felt lucky to get such a cute place with affordable rent so close to the school. She and Trent moved into the small two-bedroom house just two months ago. She was able to get the house on a section-8 plan, which really helped financially. From the time just before she delivered her baby, she had been living on state aid, plus whatever odd jobs she could pick up. She had done some baby-sitting and some sewing for the kind man who lived next door to her when they were still in the apartment. State aid was better than nothing, but it certainly didn't provide enough for anything other than the bare necessities. Food stamps, WIC, and medical coverage had been a Godsend to her.

Today was the day she began looking for employment. Other than waitress work, she had no marketable skills. She did have some business school background, but she never graduated. She had been going to school part-time when she met Jonathan and had to quit when her pregnancy began to slow her down. She retained the knowledge and the skills she had learned at the community college, so applying for an office position was an option.

Lois was pulled from her thoughts when she realized that Trent was talking to her.

"What, Honey?"

"When I get bigger will I walk to school by myself?"

"Only if you want to, Trent. Why are you asking?"

"Because those big kids over there are walking all by themselves. Their moms aren't with them."

Lois followed Trent's line of vision and saw three older boys around the age of ten, walking together, shoving each other and laughing. She glanced at Trent and saw the admiration in his eyes as he watched them. The school building loomed up ahead and she felt Trent's hand tighten around hers. Hand in hand they walked across the playground and up the steps into the school. It smelled of polish, bleach, and Lysol along with the unmistakable odor of education. Books, paper, chalk, erasers, pencils all combined had a certain smell.

"Here is your room, Trent. Room one-eighteen….the same as your birthday!"

"Hello! And who do we have here?" A melodious voice interrupted Lois.

"Trent Watkins. I'm Lois Watkins."

"Well hello, Trent. Are you ready to start school? We are going to have fun. Miss Lacey, my assistant will show you to your seat. Now let me give your mommy some papers so she knows what to expect and also how she can help us out. We have each parent bring in cookies for the class once a month. Is that agreeable to you?"

"Yes…that's fine," Lois answered.

"Now, class ends for the kindergarten at noon. We watch until all the children are picked up so try not to be late, since we have to get ready for our afternoon K-class. Oh, and if someone other than you is going to pick him up, we need to know that, and we'll have to have some ID. Here is a schedule of events, and what your child will need for each of the events. And please fill these papers out and return them tomorrow. Here are the phone numbers and email addresses you might need in case of emergencies and school closings. Let's put it all in one of our folders. All set?"

"Yes, I guess. Hug, Trent?" Lois asked as she turned to her son. He was standing there as stiff as could be, and chewing his lip. Lois knelt down and hugged him, as he fiercely hugged her back. "It's going to be okay, big guy."

"Mommy, I would still rather walk to school with you than those big kids."

"Good. I'm glad. Have a good first day of school,

my little man." She smiled and kissed his forehead before releasing him.

"Bye, Mommy," he whispered, as he raised his right hand in a wave.

Lois turned on her heel and all but ran out the door and then out of the school. The tears were like rivulets as they streamed down her cheeks and dropped onto her tee-shirt. By the time she hit the playground she was sobbing uncontrollably, and had to sit down on one of the benches provided for the faculty. Her baby was not a baby any more, and she mourned her loss. Soon he wouldn't be depending on her—wouldn't need her. But she would still need him. Forever and ever, she would need him.

...

After three days of filling out applications, handing out resumes, begging for interviews, and soaking her sore throbbing feet, the call finally came. A small insurance firm was offering her the position of file clerk, with the chance for advancement. Once she settled into the job and if they were happy with her, there was the possibility they would train her and let her study for an underwriting position. Lois was ecstatic. Now she had to make arrangements for someone to pick up Trent after school, but that shouldn't be a problem since she had so many offers from former co-workers. She would start the job the following Monday. Life was certainly looking up. She was going to be self-sufficient. She was going to support her son with a sense of pride! For the first time in a long time Lois felt like dancing.

Chapter 3

"Mommy?" Trent addressed Lois as he worked on his third grade mathematics homework at the kitchen table.

"What, Honey." She was sitting across from him, balancing her checkbook while he did his homework. They always did their work together after dinner at the kitchen table. She looked up and smiled at him and waited for his question.

"What's a....bastard?"

Lois felt a flash of heat run through her body as her heart began to pound. This was not the question she was expecting. Swallowing hard, she stared at her son.

"Where did you hear that word?" *Breathe, Lois, breathe!*

"Franklin said he couldn't invite me to his party

because his dad said he didn't want any bastards in his house....and that I was a bastard."

Lois felt her cheeks burning as the anger erupted inside of her. Who would tell a child that? What kind of a demon would condemn a little boy for his parents' actions? *Oh God! I'm going to need therapy after this!*

"Sweetheart, that is not a nice thing for Franklin's father to say." *Oh, I am so going over there!*

"But why did he say that about me?"

"He said that in error. He said it because your daddy doesn't live with us. If your daddy could be here, he would be. I'm sure of it. And you can tell Franklin that."

Lois's veins were smoldering and were about to erupt into flames. The roar inside her head was deafening. This was not going to wait! She called her friend Jackie to come and stay with Trent for a few minutes. Jackie obliged and was there in fifteen minutes. She stared at Lois quizzically.

"I'll tell you later when I get back. Want to make a pot of coffee?"

"Okay...this sounds serious."

Lois just nodded and pulled the door shut behind her.

Although it was less than a ten-minute walk, by the time Lois reached the house of the target of her anger, the anger had subsided and had turned into hurt. She blinked back the tears that were stinging her eyes, and knocked on the door. The culprit himself answered the door. She stared at him as she swallowed the lump in her throat.

"Why did you tell your son that my son is a bastard? That is a rotten thing to say about an eight-year-old boy, don't you think?"

"Lady, this whole damn neighborhood is full of traditional family units. Then you moved in. No husband, no father. We don't want our children's values and morals corrupted by some fucking whore who got herself knocked up because she couldn't let go of a man's prick."

"Oh…is that so? So instead you teach them to use profane language. Well, for your information, Trent had a father….though it's none of your business. And another thing….I don't want my son coming here anyway. The language in this house is atrocious!" And with that, Lois stormed off of the porch and jogged home.

Although she felt better after confronting Franklin's father, she knew there would be more incidents like this. People were narrow-minded and quick to judge. She couldn't protect Trent from it, and she knew eventually that day would come when he started asking his own questions about his father.

Between the time she left the house of Franklin until she reached her front door, her emotions had gone from furious, to hurt, to sadness, and to fear, ending with despair. Her heart broke for Trent and the trials before him, and her heart ached for someone to fill the void in both of their lives.

When she entered her kitchen Trent was just finishing his homework.

"All done?" She asked him.

"Yeah, it's finished. I hate doing sentences."

"No you don't. You just find doing math problems easier. Right?"

"Yeah....right," he responded.

"Now go get ready for bed and then we can have some milk and cookies before you get to bed."

"Wait, Trent....tell Mom our idea for Saturday."

"Oh....yeah!" Trent sounded enthusiastic. "Aunt Jackie wants us to go over to the ocean and see some big ships in the Navy yard. She says we can have lunch and dinner on the shore. Can we, Mommy?"

Lois looked to Jackie for clarification. "I thought it would be a nice Saturday outing. You know, get out of town for awhile."

Lois smiled for the first time since Trent asked the big question. "Yes, we can. It'll be fun. There is a small zoo there somewhere, too. Isn't there?"

"Yes, and I know exactly where it is. It's a plan?"

Lois laughed. "Yes, it's a plan. Now go get ready for bed, little man."

All smiles and grins, Trent raced toward the bathroom and his room. Lois knew it was only a temporary reprieve, but she was grateful to her friend, Jackie, nevertheless.

"He told me some kid's dad called him a bastard. He said that's where you went...down to fight the guy."

Lois laughed. "I don't think fight was exactly what I'd planned. I did confront him, though. He was just nasty and...and cruel." Lois repeated to Jackie what Franklin's father had said to her.

"What a narrow-minded jerk," Jackie responded, frowning.

"Yeah....well...we're probably going to face a lot of that over the years, so I'd better come up with some answers for my sweet son. Thanks for suggesting the trip on Saturday. That's the day of Franklin's birthday party and it will be nice to know Trent isn't sitting home doing nothing that day."

"Hey, it will be fun. I'm looking forward to it. In fact, I want to go one step further. Let's get a motel room and stay overnight on the shore. He would love that."

"Yeah! Can we, Mommy?" The women turned to see Trent standing in the doorway, grinning. He quickly took his seat and grabbed a cookie in one hand and his glass of milk in the other.

"Jackie, I'm not sure I can afford that."

"Please, Mommy? Please?"

Lois relented. "Okay, but we may have to eat hotdogs and hash for a month."

"That's okay! I love hotdogs!"

Lois smiled and then laughed. "Okay, we'll do it!"

Trent quickly slipped out of his chair and ran to Lois, wrapping his arms around her neck and hugging her tightly. "Thank you, Mommy," he whispered.

"You're welcome. Now off to bed with you. Jackie, I'll be back in a moment. I just want to tuck my little monster into bed," Lois quipped, earning a chuckle from

Trent. He loved it when she called him her Little Monster. It was a term of endearment to both of them. He usually called her the Big Monster Hunter in return.

After saying his prayers, Lois tucked him into his single bed and kissed his forehead. Trent looked into her eyes and smiled tentatively.

"Mommy? You don't think I'm a bastard, do you?"

"No, darling. I don't. Now no more on the subject...please? Just forget about it. People who say things like that are narrow-minded and...and just not very nice." She rubbed her nose on his nose in a bunny kiss and then kissed his forehead again. "I love you, Trent, and don't you ever forget it."

"I won't," he responded, as his eyelids became heavy.

She sat on the edge of his bed watching him until his breathing became shallow and even. He was asleep.

Carole McKee

Chapter 4

Lois was cleaning off her desk when the front door of the insurance office burst open. It was a blustery day, and the open door brought icy air in, causing the papers on Lois's desk to fly up and then float to the floor. A man followed the cold and then shut the door as Lois started around her desk to retrieve the papers. He stooped to help her pick them up.

"Sorry. The wind grabbed the door from me. I'm Garrett Cook. I had called earlier about insuring my cottage on the lake. Was it you I talked to? I was supposed to be here an hour ago, but traffic is horrendous. The snow is really coming down out there." He smiled at her and she returned the smile with one of her own, as she took in his solid gray eyes and well-cut dark hair. She couldn't help but notice that he was quite good looking, tall, and nicely built. Actually, he was to die for, and Lois might have died right there if she hadn't forced herself to breathe. And speak.

"I'm sorry, Mr. Cook, but you must have spoken to Helen. She is already gone for the day. She left about twenty minutes ago, but she did leave some quotes for you. I'll just turn on my computer and print them for you. I'm Lois Watkins." *It should be illegal for a man to be this good-looking.*

"Thanks, but I don't want to cause you any trouble. Besides, you should probably get going. The snow is piling up out there."

"It will only take a minute, and then I do have to leave. I don't want my son walking home in this blizzard."

"You have a son? How old is he?"

"He's ten, this coming Sunday."

"Nice. Does he look like you or your husband?"

"He looks like his father."

"Oh, well, if you two decide to have a girl someday, I would hope that she look like you."

"Is that a compliment?"

"It was meant it to be."

"Oh…well, then….thank you. But there probably won't be any more children. I'm not married," she told him as she handed him his quotes on the lake property.

Lois imagined she saw something in his eyes when she told him that, but she couldn't be sure. He took the pages from her and glanced at them before folding them and tucking them into the inside pocket of his jacket. She went around to her chair behind the desk and finished cleaning up and then turned the computer off once again. Garrett remained in front of the desk staring at her almost expectantly.

"Is there something else I can do for you, Mr. Cook?"

"Garrett, please. Call me Garrett. And yes….there is something else you can do for me. Have dinner with me sometime."

"Oh…I couldn't. It's against company policy to date our clients. I'm sorry, but thanks. I appreciate the offer."

"I wouldn't say anything."

"Mr. Cook…it's against company policy…and my policy is to maintain the well-being of my son, which includes staying employed. I apologize. Now if you'll excuse me, I really do have to lock up and go retrieve my son from school."

Garrett Cook nodded and left, allowing her to turn out the lights and lock up. The Arctic temperature caught her off guard as the wind whipped her coat and scarf around her body. Snow and sleet stung her cheeks as she trudged toward her car, and when she squinted at her car, her heart sank. Ice covered what she could see of the windshield and at least eight inches of snow covered the hood, roof, and trunk of the car. The snow around the car was piled up past the bottom of the door; making her wonder if she was going to be able to get out of the parking spot. She had to! Trent would be waiting for her at the school. He would freeze if he had to stand outside waiting for her and it would be dangerous for him to try to walk home in these conditions. Resignedly she made her way through the heavy snow toward the driver's side of the car, feeling inside her coat pocket for the little lock-heating device Trent had bought her for Christmas. It came in handy for days like this when in all likelihood, her locks would be frozen. Since she had no winter boots, her feet were already soaked through to her skin.

The lock device worked, so as she damned the weather she struggled to pull the door open through the accumulated snow on the side of the car and reached in for the ice scraper and small broom. As an afterthought, she leaned in and started the engine, silently thanking her lucky stars that the vehicle started.

"Thought you could use an extra pair of hands," a male voice came from close behind her. She flinched and then turned to see a grinning Garrett Cook, armed with a scraper and a brush.

"How thoughtful....and chivalrous. I would *love* an

extra pair of hands." In spite of the miserable cold and snow, she grinned back. As she glanced around she noticed the four-wheel jeep in front of fresh tracks in the snow. Garrett took his equipment around to the rear of the car and began scraping and brushing while Lois worked on the front. The car was cleaned off in less than half the time it would have taken her by herself, and for that she was grateful.

"Thank you so much for helping me. You have no idea how I appreciate it," she gushed from the warm interior of her Dodge.

"Well, you're welcome, but listen….I'm going to follow you in case you have any trouble. Your rear tires don't look like they have a lot of tread on them, and the front ones look a little worn, too. It's really slippery out on the roads." Garrett took note of how her rosy cheeks, red from the cold, made her green eyes look even greener.

"Well….okay. I appreciate it."

She was thinking of Trent's safety. She knew she needed new tires, but living expenses came first. She was no longer getting assistance from the government, and so all of the rent, utilities, food, clothing, medical, and car expenses had to be covered by her salary. She had moved up in the company since she began as a file clerk, but as her salary increased, so had living expenses. There was never enough money to cover everything.

Slowly she made her way up the snow and ice-covered street, glancing in her rear-view mirror. Garrett Cook was behind her. *How Thoughtful*.

She reached the school just minutes after the classes ended. Trent was standing at the curb as she pulled over to let him in. Garrett, still behind her, pulled over as well. He followed her all the way to her little house and then pulled in behind her as she fish-tailed into the short driveway. From the corner of her eye, she saw him get out of his Jeep, so she turned toward him. "Thank you, Mr. Cook. I appreciate the help. Trent, come on inside where it's warm. I'll make some hot tea for us."

Garret Cook followed them and stopped when she put her key into the lock of the front door. "Hey…do you have a snow shovel? I'll shovel this walk for you and then do some of the driveway."

"Oh…thanks, but you don't have to do that. You have done plenty already."

"Who is that man, Mommy?" Trent whispered beside her.

"Trent, this is Mr. Cook, a client from work. He was nice enough to help me clean off my car and then follow me so I didn't get stuck in the snow."

"Oh….hi, Mr. Cook. Thank you for taking care of my mom."

"It was my pleasure, Trent…and it is nice to meet you. Now…how about letting me shovel this for you while you make tea and order a large pizza with….whatever you want on it?"

"Oh…Mr. Cook…Garrett…I can't let you do that." Lois noted the disappointment on Trent's face. There was never enough money for a pizza, but even though she knew that Trent would love getting one, she couldn't allow any involvement with Garrett Cook. Not if her job might be affected by it.

"Please, Miss Watkins. I just want to wait out the traffic. You saw how bad it was out there. Now people are getting off from work. It's going to be worse. Shoveling will give me something to do while I wait it out, and then I'm going to be starved. So what do you say? Do me this favor?"

Garrett Cook's plea and the hopeful look on Trent's face whittled her down.

"Okay," she relented. "I'll order a large pizza. What do you like on it?"

"Pepperoni, but whatever you two like will be fine," Garrett stated as he reached for the snow shovel he spied leaning up against the bungalow.

Lois closed the door to keep the heat in and went to put on a pot of coffee. Garrett would certainly need something hot when he finally came inside. Trent followed his mother into the kitchen after taking off his winter gear.

"Do you like that guy, Mommy?"

"I hardly know him, Sweetie. He only followed me because my tires are bad."

"You said you needed to get new tires, but we don't have the money...right?"

"Well, right...but that's not something you need to worry about, Honey...and since this is Friday, I don't have to worry about it for a couple of days either," she assured him as she picked up the telephone to place the order for a pizza delivery.

The pizza arrived just after Garrett finished shoveling. He had shoveled the walk, and then the driveway, and completed the job by shoveling the sidewalk in front of the bungalow. He was ice cold and his clothes were soaked through to his skin. He stood just inside her front door and peeled off his boots and then his socks and hung his coat, hat, and scarf over a hook on the coat rack beside her door. He paid the delivery guy for the pizza and handed the box to Lois in exchange for the towel she held out for him to dry his hair and face. "I made a pot of coffee, so it's fresh and hot. Do you drink coffee?"

"Yes, and I'd love a cup….cream, no sugar….if you have it."

"Of course…coming right up. Uh, I wish I had some dry clothes for you to put on. Those wet pants have to be uncomfortable. You can sit over the heating duct in the kitchen if you'd like. I don't know how to thank you for helping me out like this. I really do appreciate it."

"My pleasure….but going out to dinner with me would be a way to thank me."

"Oh….I don't know…I"

"I know….it's against the company policy. I understand, but I haven't become a client yet….technically. I haven't signed any papers…."

"You should go, Mom. I can stay with Aunt Jackie. You never go anywhere, Mom. Just to work and then places with me. Aunt Jackie told me you should get to go out by yourself or with friends sometime."

"Aunt Jackie's a very wise lady," Garrett interjected.

"She's mom's best friend…and we love her. So go, Mom. Aunt Jackie will be happy if you do."

"Not to mention Garrett Cook," their guest responded. "But it can't be this weekend, because Sunday is your birthday."

"Yeah....how did you know?"

"Your mother told me. You're going to be ten....right?"

"Uh-huh. We're going to the movies and then to McDonald's after that. We never go to McDonald's so Sunday will be special. Hey....you could go with us! We're going to see the movie 'Batman.' Have you seen it yet?"

"No...I haven't."

"Want to go with us? Can he, Mom?"

"Well.....I don't know. Maybe Mr. Cook has other plans for Sunday."

"No...I don't....and I'd be delighted to go. I'll even drive since you need those tires replaced. Deal?"

Lois shrugged and agreed. After the pizza was eaten, Garrett lingered. Lois finally said goodnight to him after ten o'clock. Trent was ready to fall asleep by then. Lois had let him stay up past his bedtime since it was a Friday night and he seemed to like having Garrett there. Garrett paid attention to everything Trent said, and Trent seemed to revel in it. Lois could see where it might be important for Trent to have a male figure in his life once in a while. *And me too,* she mused to herself as she cleaned up the kitchen and turned out the lights. She slept fitfully that night and in the morning she awoke and found four brand new tires leaning against the side of her house.

Carole McKee

Chapter 5

Lois and Trent were packing clothes into their duffel bags just before dawn on the Saturday before Memorial Day. Garrett was taking them to his cottage by the lake for the three-day weekend. He had promised to teach Trent how to fish from his small cabin cruiser that was docked at the pier in front of the cottage. It would be their first visit to the cottage and their first real overnight vacation, save for the time they went to the shore with Jackie. Garrett had promised to do the cooking and the clean-up, take them fishing on the boat, and then into the small town near the lake for the spring festival that was taking place that weekend. Trent was looking forward to it, and as a matter of fact, so was she.

She and Garrett had been dating since Trent's tenth birthday. Garrett had tagged along to the movie and then to McDonald's with them and had been a part of their daily lives ever since. Lois liked him and apparently, so did Trent. He was always asking if Garrett was coming over, or was Garrett going to go with them when they went anywhere. Back in March, Garrett had helped Trent with his science project, which earned a blue ribbon at the science fair and an A in science for the year. Trent couldn't have been happier, since his project beat Franklin's project 'by a mile' as Trent put it.

Garrett had surprised Trent with a new bicycle the day after his birthday. Lois did not want to accept it, since they barely knew Garrett, but when Trent saw it, she knew it would break his heart if she made Garrett take it back. Since then, it had been one wonderful surprise after another, for both Trent and her.

On Valentine's Day she received a dozen red roses, a box of candy, and a beautiful ruby heart on a gold chain. Garrett had given Trent a gift card worth fifty dollars at Toys 'R Us. Saint Patrick's Day brought a parade and then lunch at a well-known burger place. He surprised Lois with a pair of emerald earrings. "Garrett, you're spoiling me," she had told him. "And I love doing it," he had answered back.

On Easter, Garrett was out of town visiting relatives, but before he went, he delivered a huge basket full of chocolates and sugared marshmallow treats   for the two of them, with a promise to take them out for dinner when he got back. In between those small holidays, Garrett spent a lot of time at the house, playing board games with Trent. *If the way to a man's heart was through his stomach, then the way to a woman's heart was through her child*—and Garrett had a map. Lois was definitely falling in love with him. No— Lois was already in love with him.

She hadn't just jumped into bed with him as she had with Jonathan. They had taken their time working up to that. It was right after Garrett got back from visiting his relatives at Easter that it finally happened. Trent had gone to Jackie's for the night so Lois and Garrett could go to see a play and then to dinner afterwards. Jackie had agreed to keep Trent overnight so there was no rush to get home from the dinner. Garrett had made reservations at an expensive restaurant and had insisted they go dancing after that. Lois had felt like a princess in the new dress she managed to squeeze out of the budget. Garrett held her in his arms like she was a precious item from Tiffany's as he led her around the dance floor. He had smiled down at her and her eyes reflected her feelings for him when she returned his smile. After too much wine, they kissed in the car and then headed for her place. Garrett was tender and he took his time with her that night, making her body melt into a pool of hot lava. She had savored every second of that first night of making love with him. He proved to be an excellent lover and was in tune with every part of her body and the pleasure he brought her. That night, he told her he was falling in love with her, and she almost cried with joy. Since that night, they had slept together a few more times, but never when Trent was in the house. Lois wouldn't have felt right about that and Garrett didn't press it, respecting her feelings on the matter.

A light rap on the front door brought Lois to life. He was there, and they were ready to go. Trent ran to the door and pulled it open. "Hi, Garrett...we're ready to go. I can't wait to get there."

"Good! Is your mom ready?"

"Yep! Mom!" Trent called out. "Garrett's here!"

Laughing, Lois carried the duffel bags out to the living room and dropped them at Trent's feet. "They are ready to go, Honey. Can he put them in the Jeep, Garrett?"

"Yeah, the Jeep is unlocked, so just drop them into the back of it."

"I have some other things to take. Cake, chips, cookies...." Her words were cut off by Garrett's lips as he pressed them against hers, taking full advantage of Trent being out in the driveway.

"I have a wonderful weekend planned....just the three of us. I'm hoping this is the weekend you fall in love with me." Garrett took her hands between his two palms and kissed each finger. "I want you to be mine...forever." *Was that a proposal?*

Lois smiled up at him, but said nothing. *WAS it a proposal? It sounded like it—sorta.* The moment ended with the banging of the door as Trent burst inside.

"Are we ready?"

"We sure are, Partner. I've been waiting all month for this."

"Me, too! How long does it take to get there?"

"Oh….about an hour and a half. I planned on stopping for breakfast at a pancake house on the way. They make the best banana nut pancakes and they have blueberry and chocolate, too. As a matter of fact, they have twenty-one different flavors of pancakes, so you can have your pick."

Lois grabbed the parcels from the kitchen and they headed out to the Jeep, locking the door behind them. A lump formed in her throat when she saw Trent up on Garrett's back getting a piggy-back ride to the car. *What if. She hadn't played that game in awhile.*

***

The weekend couldn't have been more perfect. The blue sky was dotted by small puffs of white clouds that reflected on the blue-green glasslike surface of the lake, which was surrounded by mountainous hills in various shades of green. Although the temperature was in the high seventies, it was probably too cool to swim, but the air was warm enough for getting some sun. Lois noticed the pink across Trent's face and back as they sat at the picnic table eating the delicious steaks prepared on the charcoal grill by Garrett. They had been on the boat all afternoon. She relaxed in a deck chair while Garrett taught Trent to fish. Her heart swelled when she remembered the look on Trent's face when he reeled in his first caught fish *ever—a trout.* He grinned from ear to ear and his eyes were wild with excitement. Garrett himself had reeled in three more and the plan was to have trout for dinner on Sunday—after Garrett scaled, cleaned and filleted them.

The cottage was another nice surprise. It had all modern appliances, including a microwave and a small stackable washer and dryer. A television stood on a pedestal along one wall. Lois had noticed a satellite dish not far from the cottage so she assumed that provided reception for the television. The furniture was comfortable and clean. The open floor plan of the living room-dining room area held a pale blue sofa and matching chair, and a pine coffee table and end table strategically placed for easy reaching. A small dinette table sat in front of a bay window overlooking the lake. The kitchen was separated from the eating area by a counter with two stools in front of it. Garrett had put Lois's things in the larger of the two bedrooms and

Trent's went into the smaller bedroom. The small bedroom held a single bed with a matching dresser. The wood looked to be oak. A gold and green comforter covered the bed. The master bedroom held a queen-sized bed with a matching dresser and nightstand. The comforter in this room was burgundy with white swirls. A burgundy winged chair stood in front of a walk-in closet. Each room had area rugs stretching almost to the baseboards, but in the master bedroom another small area rug was placed in front of a small fireplace. There was another fireplace in the living room. Trent was enthralled by the cottage, and Lois had to admit, she was, too.

"Wait until you sleep in that bed." Garrett's voice pulled her from her dreamy state as she lounged in a chair sipping a pina colada mixed especially for her. "It's one of the most comfortable beds I've ever slept in."

She smiled at him, feeling the want and desire for him flooding through her. "I think this drink is going to my head. I don't usually do this."

"I know. That's what makes it so special now." He squeezed her hand quickly and turned to Trent. "Hey, buddy....want to beat me at a game of Monopoly?"

"You have that here?"

"Yeah, I do. I have a few games here."

The darkness was creeping in fast, so they extinguished the charcoal embers and went in for the night. After a game of Clue and then a game of Monopoly, Trent's eyes were closing as he sat at the table. Lois got him into bed and shut the bedroom door quietly. Trent was asleep before his head hit the pillow. Garrett had a fire going when she came out of the small bedroom. He handed her another pina colada and pulled her down onto the sofa in front of the fire. "So how am I doing? Is my plan working? Are you falling in love with me?" He nuzzled her neck and ran his tongue along her jaw.

"Maybe," she giggled. "But I have a question. Where did all those games come from? I mean, Trent was delighted, but how did you know to have them here?"

"They came with the place. When I bought this place, it came with all the furniture, and a lot of little things. Like the games. The dishes and pots and pans were here, too. Everything I needed to just move in when I wanted."

"Hmm….what a great place."

"Yeah, it is. Now let's get back to what we were talking about."

They made love in the master bedroom and slept in each other's arms until almost daybreak. Garrett left the room with a blanket and a pillow and curled up on the sofa and slept until Trent awakened him. Together, they slipped out of the cottage and fished until noon.

Carole McKee

Chapter 6

It was just past nine in the morning when Lois heard someone knock on the front door. She had taken the day off, and Trent was in school. She knew that Garrett was probably out of town by now. He had to take a flight to Colorado early this morning since he had a business meeting at ten. In the course of the six months they had been dating, Garrett told her he was an acquisitions specialist and that he traveled a lot. It was a lucrative occupation if you didn't mind the travel, he told her.

The knock came again just as she reached the door. A well dressed woman stood on the stoop, taking Lois by surprise. Lois was still in her robe and her feet were bare. As she stared at the attractive well dressed, well coiffed woman with the flawless make-up, she began to feel inadequate, but she shrugged the feeling away.

"Yes?" She held her chin up as she stared at this

intruder.

"Are you Lois?"

"Yes. Do I know you?"

"Not yet….but you will."

"I'm sorry…I don't understand."

"I'm Victoria Cook…..Mrs. Garrett Cook."

"No….there must be some mistake."

"Yes….and you made it. You've been sleeping with my husband."

"No….that can't be. Garrett? He said he wasn't married."

"Well, he lied to you. He has been my husband for ten years. So why don't you invite me in? We have things to discuss."

Lois felt queasy and light-headed all of a sudden. She felt her world begin to cave in around her. *This can't be true! Garrett isn't married!* She stepped back, opening the door wider, allowing the woman to enter. Victoria Cook followed her out to the kitchen.

"Is that fresh coffee? If it is, may I have a cup?"

What nerve! Lois nodded and reached for a cup from the cupboard. She poured the coffee and set it down in front of the woman. "Cream and sugar?" She asked.

"Black is fine. Now let's get right to it. You will no longer be involved with my husband. I don't think I have to make it any clearer than that. I will *not* agree to a divorce...*ever.* Without me, Garrett is nothing...he owns nothing. It all belongs to me."

"Even the cottage at the lake?"

"OH...no....that shack belongs to him and that's all he has...unless you want to count the Jeep as an asset."

"Maybe that's enough."

"Enough? For who? Him or you?"

"Both of us. What about Garrett's job? He does work, doesn't he?"

"Oh yes, he works...for my father. He leaves me and he leaves his job behind. You see, Lois, I hold all the cards. Garrett is my husband, and love or no love; he will remain as my husband." Victoria Garrett stared down her nose at Lois piercing her with her cold marble-like eyes.

"Why would you want to hold on to a man who doesn't want to be with you? A man who prefers someone else?" Lois just wanted this woman to disappear, but at the same time she wanted answers to questions that she never imagined would come up. *Garrett—a married man!* She felt her breakfast begin to churn in her stomach. *I fell in love with a married man! How could this have happened?* Thoughts of Trent passed fleetingly across her mind. *What would he think? How would he feel when there was no more Garrett?* How is *she* going to feel? Right now, her body was numb with shock, but she knew that later on, when all of this sunk in, her tattered and frayed heart would be consumed with incredible pain. *Were there signs? Signs that she missed? Or signs she didn't want to see?* Somewhere from far away Victoria Cook's voice jerked her back from her thoughts.

"Pride, Lois. Something you apparently have very little of. Now you must suffer the consequences for your...indiscretion." She stood up and reached for her Gucci handbag, indicating that the discussion was over.

"H-how did you find out about me?" Lois couldn't help herself. She had to know.

"I always have my husband followed. For the past ten years he has had a tail and has never known it. You are his first affair...and to me that makes you the enemy."

She turned on her heels and strode out the front door, leaving Lois's nerve endings standing upright. Wrapping her arms around herself protectively, Lois stood rooted to the floor. She felt her hand shaking as she reached up to touch her throat. Her hand brushed the ruby heart with the gold chain that she placed around her neck the night Garrett gave it to her. Tears ran down her face as her trembling hands reached behind her neck and unclasped the chain, and then dropped it on the kitchen table. *Jackie. She needed Jackie—now.* Wiping her eyes with the back of her hand, she reached for the telephone.

Chapter 7

Jackie brought dinner when she arrived at five o'clock. Since school had ended for the year, Trent was already out riding his bike when she pulled into the driveway. Grabbing the bags of food, she hurried into the house and found Lois in a prone position on her bed.

"Tell me. Tell me everything." Her eyes were sympathetic as she sat down next to Lois and reached for her hand, noting the swollen, red-rimmed eyes.

"It just got worse. My boss at the agency just called me about fifteen minutes ago. He was furious. He fired me over the phone." Lois dabbed at her eyes with the balled up tissue she held tightly in her hand.

"Why? Didn't Garrett say he didn't insure the cottage with them because he didn't want you to get into trouble?"

"Yeah, but Mrs. Garrett has huge multi-policies with our agency. I didn't know because I didn't handle anything that big there. I handled the small stuff...car insurance, property insurance....stuff like that. Those major umbrella policy owners were handled by my boss and Helen. If I had seen the name, I might not have been blind-sided like I was."

"Wow....have you heard from Garrett?"

"No...he's in Colorado. He's not due back in town until late tomorrow night. I don't know how to get in touch with him or I would...just to warn him."

"Why? Why should you? He deceived you, Lois." Jackie immediately regretted the protest when she saw Lois begin to break down again. When Lois had called her, Jackie could barely understand what she was telling her. All she knew was that Lois badly needed her friendship and understanding right now. She reached for her hand and held on to it. "Come on....Trent will be in the house in a couple of minutes. We can't let him see you like this."

Lois sat up and swung her legs over the side of the bed as Jackie pressed a cold wet washcloth into her hand. "This should help," she told her friend.

Lois accepted the washcloth gratefully and pressed it against her eyes. She spoke as she held it there. "I'm in love with him, Jackie....and I think he loves me, too. But it has to be over now. That woman is colder than a snake. She will stop at nothing to keep what she has. I don't think there is any love there, but he is hers...like a possession. But Jackie...I have a bigger worry. Not having a job anymore...what am I going to do?"

"We'll think of something.....come on. Let's get the table set. I brought all kinds of good stuff from the deli, including Trent's favorite...peach pie."

As if on cue, they heard the front door slam and Trent's voice as he called to them. "Mom? Aunt Jackie? I'm starving!"

"Okay," they both replied in unison, and then laughed. Jackie moved first, giving Lois time to get herself together.

Dinner was the usual banter between Jackie and Trent, with Lois being unusually subdued. Trent didn't seem to notice, and Lois was glad. However, it didn't go unnoticed that Trent mentioned Garrett's name several times in the course of the meal. Not having Garrett around any more was going to have adverse effects on not just her. In just a few months, Trent had become attached to Garrett and that bond was going to be shattered, along with his little heart.

Jackie stayed until after Trent was in bed for the night. She cleaned up the kitchen while Lois tucked Trent in, and then after pouring the tea into two cups, she sat down at the table, waiting for Lois so they could talk.

"Did you hear how many times Trent mentioned Garrett?" Jackie asked her.

"Fourteen times....yes, I noticed. He's going to be devastated, Jackie. He has really become attached to Garrett. Now I know why single parents don't involve their kids when they start seeing someone. I always felt that was not very fair. The person a single parent is going out with should be exposed to the kids, and vice versa. That way, if they decide to make it permanent, there are no surprises. But now I can see where that may be cause for major disappointment. I just could never imagine not involving Trent in what I do or where I go."

"I know, Lois. And I always thought that was a *good* thing. You love your kid, and you want to share everything with him. I don't see anything wrong with that."

"Except now...when he's going to be very disappointed...and hurt."

"Maybe he won't ask any questions."

"Yeah, and maybe the oceans will dry up," Lois responded.

"Well, there is no sense worrying about it until you

talk to Garrett, so now let's think about what you're going to do for work. What exactly did your boss say?"

"Well, apparently Victoria Cook went straight to the office from here, foaming at the mouth. She said if I was going to remain employed there she would cancel all of her policies and take her business elsewhere. He had no choice, and he is including a severance package in with my last pay and I can keep my medical coverage for ninety days. That's a plus. Also, my vacation pay will be included so I have at least two months to find another job."

"Well, that's actually good. You can take some time to find a decent position somewhere, and you can be home with Trent for most of the summer. I take it he really didn't want to let you go?"

"No...he didn't....but she has such clout. Her father has insurance policies there, too. Keeping me would have bankrupted the agency."

"How does one get such clout?"

"I don't know....but the point is....I'm not the villain here. I'm a victim. Garrett said he was not married...he's the villain. Victoria and I are victims. Why am I paying the consequences?" Lois began to break down again. "I love him, Jackie. How could I love a cheat? And a Liar?"

"Did he actually tell you he wasn't married?" Jackie

asked.

"No...I guess he really didn't say he wasn't married, but I just assumed...since he was here a lot and even on holidays and weekends. I wonder how he pulled that off."

"Well...that is something you should ask him. Maybe Victoria is not being honest with you. Maybe they are separated...or have an open marriage....or something."

"I am really worried about how Trent is going to take all of this. He is so attached to Garrett. Oh, Jackie....that man was wonderful to both of us."

"I could see that, Lois. That time he came here and brought you that cake...the day I met him...he seemed so kind and gentle. He was sweet...very sweet."

"And now I have to let him go," Lois whispered tearfully.

Chapter 8

Trent was already asleep when Lois heard the tapping on the front door. It was after ten, so it could only be one person—Garrett. She grabbed hold of her self-control and stiffly walked to the door to open it.

"Hi, Honey...I'm home," Garrett teased.

"I'd say I'm the wrong woman to say that to...don't you think?"

"Why do you say that? Who else would I say it to?"

"Your wife, maybe?"

Garrett was visibly shocked. "My wife?"

"Yes, your wife. Victoria's secret has been revealed, Garrett. She was here, and then she was at my job. She got me fired. Fired, Garrett...as in I now have no income. Thanks a lot." Lois turned away when she realized that she was going to cry.

"Lois, I…"

"You what? Don't know what to say? I guess you don't. Why, Garrett? Why? Why did you pursue me knowing you had no right to? You caused me to go against all of my principles, my rules. I would never have gone out with you if I knew you were married."

"Lois…I don't love my wife. I never loved her. I married her because she was pregnant. She lost the baby after we were married. I wanted a divorce or an annulment way back then, but she refused. She always held it over my head that I worked for her father. Lois, I love you….and I love Trent. I've been driving myself crazy just trying to figure out how to be with you forever."

"In order to do that, you have to be free, Garrett. You are not. You are married and I don't think I can forgive you for what you have done. Not only did you deceive me and make me fall in love with you, but you made my son fall in love with you. Aside from my hurt and disappointment, what about his? Do you have any idea how attached to you he has become? He talks about you all the time when you're not here. He is going to be devastated when you aren't coming around any more."

"Lois, don't cut me out of your life…please. I'll be devastated if I can't see you and Trent any more.

Please...let me try to work this out."

"Garrett, please go. If and when you get a divorce, you can come back. I'll be here. But as long as you are married and I know it, you cannot come back here. Now please leave, Garrett. Leave." She almost retracted when she saw the pain in his eyes.

As he stared into her eyes and took note of the set jaw, he realized that she was serious. There was nothing he could do but leave. He turned and walked toward his Jeep, his shoulders sagging. *Don't go! Stay! Beg me!* It was all Lois could do to keep from calling him back. Her chest heaved up and down as she shut the door and locked it. Covering her mouth to smother the sobs, she ran to her room and flung her body onto the bed and cried herself to sleep.

It was daylight when Trent came into her room to awaken her.

"Mom? I'm hungry. Can we have breakfast now?"

"Yes, Trent....give me a moment to get up. I have a headache, Honey."

"Okay...I'll wait in the kitchen for you. Do you want me to get you some Tylenol?"

"No, Sweetie.....that's okay." Lois dragged herself off of the bed and headed toward the bathroom. She winced at her reflection in the bathroom mirror and then cupped her hands under the cold tap water and splashed her face with it. She hurt everywhere. *'Did emotional pain affect everyone physically, or am I a rarity?'* She wondered as she moved her aching bones toward the kitchen where Trent was waiting for breakfast.

"How about French Toast this morning?"

"Okay...yeah....that's sound great, Mom." *When did he start saying mom instead of mommy?* "Is Garrett coming over today?"

Here it comes. The moment we have been waiting for. "No, Honey, Garrett won't be coming over today." Lois tried to make her voice sound matter-of-fact.

"Why not? He came home last night, didn't he?"

"Well, yes....but he won't be here today, Trent."

"Then when?"

The moment of truth. "Trent, Garrett may not ever come back here again." Lois tried to keep her voice steady and calm.

"Why?"

"Well, he probably won't be able to."

"Did he die?"

"No….no, Honey….nothing like that." *Where would he get an idea like that?*

"Then what? Why won't he be able to come here?"

Lois couldn't tell Trent that Garrett had a wife who wouldn't let him come back but she couldn't think of anything else to say, so she remained silent.

"You made him go away! It's *your* fault!" Trent lashed out. "I hate you! Did you make my dad go away, too? I hate you! I hate you!"

Trent jumped up and ran from the table. Lois was stricken as she heard his bedroom door slam. What had just happened? Trent never spoke to her like that. *Hate her! NO! He can't hate her!* She covered her face with her hands and rested her elbows on the table. The pain is now a double-edged sword. *Garrett is gone and now Trent hates me.* Without thinking, she reached for the telephone and called Jackie.

Carole McKee

Chapter 9

It was past noon when Trent came out of his room. He refused to look at Lois as he walked past her and out the front door. She watched him from the window as he sulked up the sidewalk with his shoulders slumped and his hands stuffed into his pockets. Lois felt a stab in her heart as she watched. He was hurting, but so was she! Garrett had been wonderful to them, but it was Garrett who cheated; it was Garrett who deceived her; and it was Garrett who caused her to lose her job! It wasn't fair that Trent was treating her like the villain here.

Jackie arrived around three in the afternoon. Lois had not seen Trent since he walked out the door three hours ago, and she was beginning to panic. He was still her little boy, even if he did hate her at the moment.

"I'll go look for him. You stay here and bake something. I'm sure he's hungry so I'm going to offer a trip to McDonald's and then he and I can talk." Jackie stared at her friend for a moment. "Is that okay?"

"Yeah...sure, Jackie. I think I have enough ingredients to bake some peanut butter cookies. What are you going to say to him?"

"Nothing devastating....just that grownups don't always have happy endings. That you wanted that happing ending with Garrett but you can't have it. No details," she assured Lois.

Lois nodded her approval and reached for the flour canister. Jackie slipped out the front door and began walking, looking both ways for Trent. She found him sitting on a swing in the park, twisting the chains of the swing around and then lifting his feet and letting the chair of the swing spin around as he stared at the ground.

"Yo, Trent! Hi there!" She yelled as she ran up on him. "What are you up to?"

"Nothing....just swinging," he mumbled.

"Looks to me like you're spinning....not swinging."

"Yeah, I guess. Did my mother send you to look for me?"

"No, Honey....she didn't. I came looking for you on my own. How about going to McDonald's with me? I'm hungry for a Big Mac."

As much as Trent wanted to say no, he couldn't because he was starving. He knew if he went, Aunt Jackie would want to talk about him and his mother. He didn't. Garrett wasn't coming back and that was his mother's fault, as far as he was concerned. But the hunger overtook the anger, so he nodded and stood up to go with her. The ride to McDonald's was a silent one. Inside the restaurant, Jackie chose a booth far away from most of the patrons and set the tray down. She watched as Trent dug into the food and began wolfing it down.

"Hey, slow down. You'll make yourself sick." Jackie warned. "So tell me what's wrong."

"Garrett won't be coming back...that's what's wrong. My mother made him go away."

"Why do you say your mother made him go away?"

"Because.....Garrett liked us. He wouldn't just go away on his own." Trent's tone was full of all the conviction a ten-year-old boy could muster.

"Trent....you don't know what happened. Your mother didn't do anything wrong. She's hurting, too....maybe even more than you are...or maybe in a different way. I know you cared a lot for Garrett, but so did your mother. It hurt her. It hurt her really bad to let him go...but she had to."

"Why?"

"That's between grown-ups, Honey....but when you get older, maybe she will tell you and you will understand. But what is even worse, Honey....is now you have hurt her, too. Believe me, Sweetie, she did what was right, and for that you hate her. That's not very fair. She doesn't deserve that."

"So I should say I'm sorry?"

"No, not necessarily....just don't shun her. When I left the house she was crying and making peanut butter cookies for you. You're a pretty lucky kid to have a mother who would do that after you treated her like you did."

"I guess. My mom was crying?"

"Uh-huh."

"Can we go home now?"

"Uh-huh."

The car ride was another silent one. Trent was out of the car as soon as it came to a complete stop. He ran inside, threw his arms around Lois, and hugged her tightly. "Don't cry any more, Mom. I still love you."

Although that was supposed to stop her from

crying, Lois sat down and cried harder, totally confusing Trent. She hugged him back. "Thank you, Trent," was all she could say. She was just glad to have her son back.

On the surface, things appeared to return to normal. Trent was once again the darling child Lois adored, and the peace and harmony in the house was restored. But Trent had not forgiven her. A deep resentment began to grow inside of him. Two men—his father and Garrett—had been in his mother's life. They were both gone. What did she do to make them go away?

Carole McKee

Chapter 10

"Are you up, Trent?" Lois called from the hallway. "Come on, big guy...it's your first day of middle school."

"I'm up, Mom," he responded.

"Want scrambled eggs for breakfast?"

"Yeah, that's fine. Did you iron my new shirt?"

"Yup...sure did. It's hanging outside your door."

"Thanks," Trent shouted through the closed bedroom door.

Lois smiled to herself. He was growing up so fast. It seemed like it was only yesterday that he was toddling around, following her through the rooms of the old apartment. She went back to the kitchen and began making his breakfast. He came out of his room and dropped onto a kitchen chair, dressed and ready, just as she was sliding the eggs onto a plate.

"Do you want me to drive you to school today...since it's the first day?"

"Yeah, sure...that'd be great."

"So go on and eat and I'll throw some clothes on."

"Aren't you working today?"

"No...I took the day off."

"Oh," he responded, and then picked up his fork. Lois caught a look in Trent's eyes that she had never seen before, and she wondered what it meant. Shrugging it off, she ran to her room and quickly changed into a pair of jeans and a tee-shirt. When she came back Trent was ready to go.

"Why did you take today off?" He asked.

"Because the carpet cleaners are coming this afternoon. I have to pick everything up and move it out of the living room and the bedrooms. All three rooms are going to be cleaned."

"Did you tell me this before?"

"I'm not sure, Honey. Why?"

Because I could have helped you."

"Oh, that's okay, Honey. I can get it all. Is there

anything in your room that has to be picked up other than the furniture?"

"No, just my shoes. Do you want me to put them in my closet before we go?"

"Well, sure. That would be good. Here is money for lunch. I'll put it on the table by your book bag."

"Okay," he answered as he disappeared into his room. Within moments he was back and they were ready to go.

This was the first day Lois had asked to have off since she began working at the new job. It had taken her several months to find this position and by the time she did, the bills were all backed up and way overdue. The salary was not as good as her salary had been at the last job, but she would be able to work herself back up to a better paying position again. She was still playing catch-up on the bills, but she was managing. Although she went without a lot of things, she made sure Trent had whatever he needed. She knew there were things that he wanted—things she couldn't give him—but he had what he needed.

Since the flair-up over Garrett, it seemed that Trent had called a truce. Lois could tell that there had been a change in Trent, but at least he didn't seem to hate her any more. She was sure Jackie had helped with that one.

Even though neither she nor Trent ever mentioned Garrett's name, she knew that he still missed him. *She* missed him. She wondered where he was and what he was doing. Did he ever get a divorce? Was he trying to make a go of it with his wife? Was he seeing someone else? That question caused a painful jab in her heart. Late at night when Trent was sound asleep, she still lay in bed thinking about Garrett. She played the old 'what if' game. What if he came back? What if he got his divorce? What if he came and begged her to take him back? What then? Then the game turned into her mind movie—a sweet story of a long lost love returning, and another happily ever after ending, mentally written and produced by screenwriter-producer Lois Watkins.

"Mom? Did you hear what I asked you?" Trent's voice interrupted her thoughts.

"Oh, no....I'm sorry, Trent. I must have been daydreaming. What did you say?"

"I asked if it was okay if I went to a friend's house after school. I saw Jason Blake yesterday and we are going to be in the same homeroom. He asked if I wanted to come over after school today and hang out."

"Well....I suppose that would be fine. Just be home by six. We're going to have spaghetti for dinner, and I know you like that. So just be home by six, okay?"

"Sure," Trent complied.

"You have your lunch money?"

"Yep, I got it."

"Okay….have a great day, little man…and I'll see you later." Lois swung the car up to the curb and stopped. Trent grabbed his nearly empty book bag as he unfastened his seatbelt, and was out of the car in a flash. *No kiss? Are we too old for that already?* Lois sighed and hurried home in order to get the place ready for the carpet cleaners. Hopefully they would be in and out and the carpets would be dry by the time Trent came home from his friend's house.

Carole McKee

Chapter 11

Trent zipped up his almost-full book bag and ran to catch up with his buddy Jason. They started walking toward Jason's house before they spoke to each other.

"So what are you up for today?" Jason asked him. "Want to shoot some hoops in my yard?"

"You have a hoop in your back yard? Cool!"

"Yeah...my dad put it there before he took off with his girlfriend."

"Oh...wow...so he doesn't live with you?"

"No....not any more. My mom says she hopes he dies a painful death."

"Why would she say that?"

"Because....he left us and doesn't even call to see how we are. He doesn't give my mother any money to help pay the bills either. My mom is taking him to court."

"My dad doesn't live with us, either. I don't even know him. My mom says he doesn't even know about me."

"Why didn't your mom tell him? Maybe he wants a kid."

"I don't know why. She says she doesn't know where he is. I asked her about him a couple of times, but she doesn't like to talk about it."

Jason nodded as he reached down for the key that was kept hidden in a fake rock under the front step. He unlocked the door, let them both enter, and then he locked the door behind him.

"Come on in my room. My mother works until five and then she gets home about five-thirty. How long are you allowed to stay?"

"I have to be home by six…for spaghetti dinner…my favorite."

"At least your mom cooks. We eat a lot of sandwiches because my mom is always so tired when she comes home. I like it when she makes grilled cheese sandwiches though. Does your mom work?"

"Yeah, she does, but she's off today. She always makes a big meal when she's off work. Then she freezes some of it and we can have it another night."

"That's pretty cool. Maybe I'll tell my mom about that."

"You don't have any brothers or sisters?" Trent asked.

"Yeah, I have a sister. She's never here...always with her boyfriend somewhere....screwing. I heard my mother say that."

Trent just nodded. He really wasn't sure what Jason meant by that. He filed it away until he could figure out what it meant.

Jason's hand fumbled around inside a drawer in his bureau and pulled out half a pack of cigarettes. He held them up for Trent to see. "Want a cigarette?"

"NO...I mean, I don't smoke." Trent grinned sheepishly, not wanting Jason to think he was some kind of a nerd or sissy.

"Did you ever?"

"No, not really. My mom doesn't smoke, so where would I get them?"

"Steal 'em. That's what I do when I can't find my mother's cigarettes. I take 'em from my mother's friends or the neighbor. He doesn't hide 'em very well."

Jason sat down on the side of his bed and put a cigarette between his lips, struck a match and put it to the tobacco end of the filtered cigarette. He drew in deeply, like he had been doing it for years. He tossed the pack to Trent and watched. Trent hesitated and then picked up the pack. He had never even imagined smoking a cigarette. His mom didn't smoke, and neither did Aunt Jackie. *Or Garrett.*

"What the hell....why not." *Maybe my dad smoked.* Trent pulled one out of the pack and stuck it in his mouth. Jason tossed him the book of matches, and he lit his cigarette, imitating Jason's actions, and then he began to choke.

Jason squealed with laughter, doubled over, holding his stomach. "You'll get used to it," he laughed. "That first drag is the worst. You okay?"

Trent nodded. "Can I have something to drink?"

Jason ran to the kitchen and pulled two soda cans out of the refrigerator.

"Are you okay?" He asked as he handed one can to Trent. "Just take it slow. Don't suck it in very hard."

Trent nodded and then drank from the can. He looked at the cigarette he still held between his two fingers, still lit, and took another small drag on it. This time he didn't cough. He watched Jason pull the smoke from his cigarette into his lungs, envious because he

wasn't able to do that. *He was acting like a baby*.
"Won't your mother smell the cigarettes?"

"She won't notice. She'll probably have one in her
mouth when she walks in anyway, so she won't smell
mine. I'll open a window just in case."

Trent watched the smoke from the room pour out
through the opened window, and thought about that
going into his lungs. *Who cares?* He brushed the
thought aside and when Jason offered him another one;
he took it and lit it.

He and Jason sat in Jason's room, talking and
smoking, until it was almost time for Jason's mother to
get home. Trent walked the six blocks to his home and
was there in plenty of time for dinner.

"I smell cigarettes," Lois commented.

"Yeah, Jason's mother smokes." He wasn't lying, he
rationalized. She *did* smoke.

He went into the bathroom and washed his hands
and face and then brushed his teeth and used
mouthwash before he went out to the kitchen.

"She must be a chain-smoker...one after another. I
can really smell the smoke on you."

"Yeah, she is, but her friend was there smoking

them, too. Jason and I were in the bedroom but we could still smell it."

That seemed to satisfy Lois's curiosity about the smell of cigarettes, because she let the subject drop. "Ready to eat?" She asked.

"Yeah, I'm starved. The carpets look nice, Mom."

"Yes, they do," she agreed and smiled at him. "Now tell me about your first day of middle school.

Chapter 12

Lois was, once again, underwriting small insurance policies for the agency she went to work for after the fiasco with Garrett and his wife. Although she still thought about Garrett from time to time, she no longer longed for him as she once had. She and Trent did not mention his name, and so the chapter on Garrett Cook was closed.

She smiled at the couple sitting in front of her desk, and then handed them their home owner's policy and a pen, pointing to the signature lines. "If you will sign right there, we can have you on your way in a moment," she told them. She watched as they placed their signatures on the proper lines, and then she retrieved the policy, made a copy, and then folded their original, and placed it in the special insurance agency envelope with brochures and coupons attached. She stood and extended her hand as they gathered their things and got up from the chairs they sat in. Smiling, she thanked them for their business and told them to give her a call if there was anything else she could do for them.

As the clients closed the door behind them, the receptionist handed Lois a phone message that was marked 'of high importance.' Lois quickly read the message and grabbed up the telephone and dialed the school. The number was a direct line to the principal's office. Lois counted the rings impatiently, tapping her fingers on her desk and sighing. Finally, someone answered.

"Principal Phillips speaking," the annoyed male voice boomed through the receiver.

"Mr. Phillips, this is Lois Watkins. You called?"

"Yes, Mrs. Watkins....I have Trent here in my office and I would like for you to come here and pick him up. He will start a three-day suspension starting tomorrow, but we need to speak to you today."

"I'll be there in less than an hour." Lois hung up and went to tell her co-worker she was leaving for the day.

She made a conscious effort to obey the speed limits as she drove toward the middle school. *What could Trent have done?* The principal sounded really angry. Trent was now in his last year of middle school, due to start high school in the fall, and this was the first time she had ever gotten a call from the principal. She found a parking spot, locked her car, and went in through the main doors toward the administrative offices. The secretary gave her a grim smile and told her to go in. Inside the principal's office, Trent and his friend Jason sat side by side in straight-backed chairs, the principal sat behind his desk, and a police officer stood just inside the door. Lois's heart dropped to her knees. She could feel her pulses pounding and immediately, her deodorant quit working.

"What's this all about?" She asked immediately.

"Please have a seat, Mrs. Watkins," The police officer indicated an empty chair. "We're waiting for Jason's parent to show up before we proceed."

Lois turned to stare at Trent and saw no reaction on his face as he stared blankly back at her. She watched as he and Jason exchanged a look that was somewhere between a smirk and a smile. The room was quiet except for the squeak of the leather on the principal's chair, and the scrape of the boy's shoes on the floor. The police officer quietly coughed into his hand. Outside the room, new sounds erupted and a voice was raised. "My mom," Lois heard Jason whisper just as the door opened.

"Mrs. Blake, have a seat, please," Principal Phillips

pointed to the last empty chair in the room, waited for Jason's mother to sit, and then cleared his throat.

"I called you parents in here today because your sons are being charged with vandalizing the school." His head swiveled toward Lois and his hawk-like eyes focused on her when he heard her gasp. "These two vandals spray-painted a few four-letter words on the walls of the bathrooms, using red spray paint."

Lois not only gasped again, but she began to feel like she was going to faint. *Trent? My God! When did he begin doing things like this?* She felt like she should say something, but she couldn't get past the ping pong ball lodged in her throat. Clasping her hands tightly, she stared back at the principal waiting for him to continue; but the police officer took over.

"Vandalizing is a misdemeanor, but there are consequences for it. The damage must be paid for, and the boys will be suspended. If we can settle it here right now there is no need to have a hearing. This will go on their record, nevertheless. Now this is Trent's first offense, but Jason...we have had a couple of run-ins in the past. So Jason, this is your last chance. One more time, and you're facing juvie...you got that?"

Jason nodded as he continued to stare at the floor.

"Now I understand that both of you are single parents....is that correct?" This time it was the principal speaking. Both Lois and Jason's mother, Rita Blake confirmed that information. "Well, the damage will have to be paid for. I strongly suggest you get in touch with the fathers for help with this. It's going to be expensive to remove that red paint and then repaint the walls."

Lois nodded but said nothing. *Expensive. Like every other consequence in her life.* She reeled her thoughts back in and focused on what Mr. Phillips was saying.

"These two boys will not be allowed back into school until next Monday. At that time, they will spend the next month in after-school detention. When the walls in the bathrooms are repainted, the school will send you the invoices. You will each be responsible for half of each invoice. Is that understood?" Both mothers nodded.

"And I think it would behoove both of you to figure out a way to make your sons pay for the damages. Make them get a paper route or make them sell their play stations. That is all…have a nice day."

The chairs scraped the floor as everyone stood up. Rita Blake grabbed Jason by the arm and yanked him out of the room, while Lois turned to stare at Trent. She bit down on her bottom lip to keep from crying as she nodded toward the door. She followed him out and they walked to her car in silence. *Play station? Like I could afford for Trent to have one of those.*

She waited until he had his seatbelt in place before she put the key in the ignition. The car chose that moment to protest her attempt and almost didn't start. After a small backfire, the engine finally came to life.

"We need a new car, Mom."

"Yes, Trent...we do. But I guess I'll be buying paint instead."

The ride home was made in silence. When they got through the front door, Trent turned to Lois. "Mom, I'm sorry."

"Just go to your room, Trent...please," she sighed as she sagged down onto a kitchen chair and rubbed her temples. *How am I going to pay for damages to the school when I can barely cover my bills now?* Lois bit down hard on her lip to keep from crying, but the tears won out. *What was happening? Was there something she wasn't doing for Trent? He has always been a terrific kid!* Anger and frustration nipped at her as she scrubbed the tears from her cheeks with her palms. The sound of the telephone interrupted her roiled brain and she jumped up to grab it. Thank God it was Jackie.

Lois returned to work the next morning while Jackie stayed at the house with Trent. Since she could work from home on her laptop, she agreed to stay at Lois's until Trent's suspension was over. There was going to be a very long discussion between her and Trent while Lois was at work. What was wrong with him? He knew how his mother struggled. *And he also knew how much Lois loved him.*

Trent had spent the evening in his room, only coming out when Lois called him to dinner. Thunderous silence filled the kitchen as Lois, Jackie, and he ate the dinner Lois had prepared, and he immediately returned to his room when he finished eating. Long after Trent was in bed sleeping, Jackie and Lois talked about what type of punishment should be handed down. Lois had never punished Trent before; there was never a need. She hated to do it now, but she knew that it was necessary. Of course, there would be no more allowance until the debt was paid, and Jackie suggested that Lois ground him. No phone, no television, and no going anywhere for a month. That sounded reasonable to Lois. She would tell him when she came home from work today.

Carole McKee

Chapter 13

"Jason said his dad is a piece of shit," Trent informed Lois on the way to school on his first day back after the suspension. Lois had to take a couple of hours off that morning in order to get him back into school. Although they were speaking, the tension between the two of them was thick. Trent had accepted his punishment, but he was not real happy about it. Suddenly, as if overnight, the closeness they had always shared was gone—and it broke Lois's heart.

"That's not nice for him to say that." Lois responded.

"Yeah, well...the point is...he can say it....because he knows his dad. I can't say that. I have no idea what my dad is like."

"He is not a piece of sh—crap, Trent. He was a very nice man, as I remember."

"Then why didn't he stick around?"

"Because...he just didn't. I've already told you....he didn't know anything about you, or he may have stayed."

"Why don't you ever talk about him? Why don't you tell *me* anything about him? Mom, because I don't know anything about my father, I really don't know who I am!"

'Trent...you're...Trent, you are my son. I love you. Your father left town before I knew I was going to have you. He...was traveling on business when I met him. We had a special time together and then he had to go. I tried to contact him. I wrote him a couple of letters but I didn't hear back from him. Maybe," Lois sighed. "Maybe he moved and never got the letters."

"Or maybe the address he gave you was bogus."

"Since the letters weren't returned as undeliverable, I don't think he gave me a bogus address. He may have.....I don't know....maybe he got married to someone else. The address he gave me was his mother's address. She may have just thrown the letters away. I don't know. I just don't know, Trent. I'm sorry."

Lois made a right into the parking lot of the school. "I have to go in with you to sign you back in. Look....We'll talk about this later. I promise."

Trent nodded and let the subject drop, but Lois knew it wasn't over. Trent was going to bombard her with questions that demanded answers—answers she didn't have.

"Do you want me to pick you up after detention?"

"I guess. We should get out at four-fifteen."

"I'll be here….unless the car breaks down." Lois assured him as he pulled open the double doors leading to the administration offices, holding one open for her to pass through.

Lois met with the principal for the second time. This second meeting was a reinstatement interview in order for Trent to get back into classes. When Trent was released and ordered back to class, there were some papers that Lois needed to sign before she left the school. As she was signing them, the police officer who was handling the vandalizing charge approached her.

"Mrs. Watkins isn't it?" His inquiry was polite and subtle.

"Yes, Officer….hello. I just brought Trent back to school and after I sign these papers I have to get to work." She hoped she didn't sound rude or abrupt. She really *did* have to get to work.

"Well, I won't keep you. I just wanted a moment of your time."

Lois finished the paperwork and handed it to the clerk behind the counter as her eyes shifted up toward the police officer's face. "What can I do for you, Officer…Hanley?" She spoke his name after looking at his name tag.

"Well…listen….Trent seems like a pretty good kid."

"He is…or at least he has been up until this incident," she responded.

"I just wanted to advise you that it might be a good idea to keep him away from Jason Blake. The kid has been in trouble since he started middle school. I would hate to see him drag Trent down."

"Thank you for letting me know. I'll see what I can do about breaking them up. I know very little about Jason. He has only been at the house a couple of times, and the first time I met his mother was here the other day. I appreciate your concern."

"No problem," he answered quickly, and then hesitated. "Let me walk you to your car."

Before Lois could protest, he placed his hand on her elbow and nudged her toward the outside doors. "How involved in Trent's life is his dad?"

"Not involved at all. I don't even know where he is."

"Hmm…deadbeat. I guess you get no child support

either, then…do you?"

"No….no support of any kind, and I might add that it's very tough raising a child alone. I love my son, but it sure would be nice to have a little help once in awhile."

"Maybe I can help. I run an after school program for at-risk kids. You know…kids who have problems at home, or create problems at home and at school. I've had a lot of success with it."

Lois suddenly became very interested in what Officer Hanley was saying. "What do you do with these kids?"

"Well, we play basketball or volleyball…..sometimes soccer. There is a reading room for kids to read or do homework, and of course, I'm available to help them with that. They can draw or do other artwork….whatever they like to do. It keeps them off the streets and keeps them from becoming involved in mischief."

"That sounds nice. I'll talk to Trent and see if he's interested. Where is this place?"

"It's right next to the police station. In fact, the building belongs to the city, and is used and run by the police department. Some of the other guys volunteer their time when they can, but usually it's just me. Why don't you come by and check it out for yourself?"

Lois nodded, thinking it sounded like it would be a good thing to get Trent involved in. As she unlocked her car door, Officer Hanley spoke again.

"There's something else I wanted to ask you. Would you have dinner with me sometime?"

"No," she retorted quickly. "I can't."

"Are you involved with someone?"

"Yes...my son, and for now that's plenty. Have a good day, Officer." She smiled and shut the car door, putting the car in gear immediately. As she drove away, she saw him standing there staring after her car. She hoped he wasn't memorizing the license plate or noticing some violation that he could ticket her for. Then she remembered—he's a school police officer. They don't write tickets for auto violations.

Chapter 14

"You're not going to make me go there, are you, Mom?"

"No, Trent....of course not. If you don't want to go you don't have to. I was just telling you about it to see if you would be interested."

"Well, I'm not."

"Okay...I just thought it might be nice to have somewhere to go to play soccer or basketball, or even have a room to do homework. Be with other kids instead of just Jason. You know...expand your horizons, and all that."

"You don't like Jason, do you?"

"I hardly know him, Honey. I just think you should have more friends than just one. And besides, maybe you would like to learn how to play a sport. It couldn't hurt."

"Did that cop hit on you?"

"What? Why would you ask that?" Lois felt the heat crawl up the back of her neck. It was almost as though Trent was psychic, or did he know something?

"I saw the way he was staring at you last week when I got suspended. He looked like a hungry dog looking at a steak. He did, didn't he?"

"Oh Trent, that's absurd. No, he didn't. Not exactly."

"Jason thinks you're hot."

"Jason shouldn't be thinking anything like that about your mother, Trent. Why would he even say that anyway?"

"Well, because....for a mother you *are* pretty good-looking."

Lois laughed quietly. "Thank you, my favorite son."

"So I don't have to go to that after-school thing...right?"

"No, you don't have to go. But Trent...I think you should start thinking about your choices. It's important that when you have to decide something that you think about what consequences it will bring. Choose what is the best thing to do, even though it may not be as much fun, or it may be unpopular with your peers, or not very cool. Success in life is not always about fun, popularity, or being cool. It's about making right choices."

The rest of the ride home was in silence. Lois was lost in her own thoughts about how much Trent knew about things like dating, attraction, and sex. He was only twelve, but it seemed kids grew up faster these days. She mulled it over in her mind about how she should approach the subjects. She really wished she had a man's help with this. *Like maybe Garrett or Jonathan.*

"What are we having for dinner? I'm hungry."

"Toad stools and rat's feet."

"Great!" He laughed. "My favorite," he teased, warming Lois's heart.

Lois continued to pick Trent up after detention for the rest of the week. It seemed as though they were getting back on good ground with each other, which was a relief to Lois. Trent has been so polite and accommodating all week, so Lois swung into the drive-thru of McDonald's and placed a large order for the two of them. She could tell Trent was happy about it.

"So is this one of those good choices you keep

talking about?" Trent asked, with just a hint of humor in his voice.

"Well....yes," she responded, just a little surprised at the question. "See, this is a choice I made and it makes both of us happy and nobody gets hurt...except for a few clogged arteries, I suppose. But yes, this is what I'm talking about. No harm, no foul...and everybody's happy. Not all good choices are unpleasant."

Trent carried the bags of food inside while Lois gathered the mail out of the mailbox. The bill for the paint and repair of the school bathroom walls was among the other envelopes. She set everything aside and just set the table. She didn't want to ruin the mood by opening the envelope. The expense was going to really set her back, she was sure. All through the meal, she and Trent chatted about school, his classes, and his grades. Although he was making average marks for the most part, she had hoped he would take his classes more seriously and plan on going to college...though God only knew how she would swing that. She had been putting money away for him, but so far the account had only accumulated a little less that four hundred dollars—not even the cost of one college course. She realized she had four more years to save, and then of course there would be financial aid. The possibility of Trent going to college was definitely there, but he had to want it, and work for it.

When they had finished eating, Trent began to remove the empty plates and bags from the table, while Lois put on a pot of coffee. Tonight would be just a night of relaxation for her. There was plenty of time to open her mail in the morning. Maybe they could rent a movie if there wasn't anything good on television. Trent was still grounded but Lois didn't feel that a movie should be out of the question since he had been so pleasant to be around all week.

Just as the coffee finished brewing, Lois was surprised by a knocking on the door. She wasn't expecting anyone this evening. Jackie sometimes popped in when she had no other plans, but Jackie was out of town visiting her brother until Sunday.

"I'll get it," Trent offered. Lois nodded.

As she dried her hands on a tea towel, she heard a man's voice and then Trent's voice. She could hear the resentment and the hostility in Trent's voice so she quickly moved from the kitchen to the living room. Officer Hadley stood just inside the house, filling up the door space. "Officer Hadley...what brings you here?" Lois asked almost breathlessly. *Oh no...more trouble?*

"May I come in? I just wanted to touch base with you about what we talked about." *And ask you out again.*

"Come in. Would you like a cup of coffee? I just made a pot."

"We don't have any donuts," Trent piped up.

Officer Hadley chuckled. "It may surprise you, Trent, but I don't eat donuts. I watch my weight and my cholesterol." Trent made no comment.

Lois pulled two cups out of the cupboard and filled them with coffee. She got the sugar and the powdered creamer out and set them on the table. From the corner of her eye she saw Trent leaning against the door frame, his arms folded, waiting to see if he was going to be dismissed. *No, my son, you are not going to be dismissed.*

"Trent, do you want a glass of milk?" Lois asked as she placed cookies on a plate and set the plate in the center of the table. She could see the disappointment on Officer Hadley's face and she was glad she had included Trent. *Wasn't this supposed to be about Trent?* Trent took the hint and with a look of smugness on his face, accepted the glass of milk and plunked himself down in a chair across from Officer Hadley. Lois took a seat, too. She managed a quick smile at the officer.

"Now what is it you want to talk about, Officer Hadley?" She kept her voice quiet and gracious as she looked him in the eye.

"Well, have you thought about Trent joining my

after school program?"

"Yes, I have. Trent isn't interested, so he won't be joining."

"Mrs. Watkins, it's a great program. He would benefit from it."

"Well, not if he's not interested, he wouldn't. It would be senseless to force him to go to something he isn't interested in doing."

"But he doesn't know if he would like the program or not if he doesn't try it." The officer appeared to be frustrated.

"May I ask a question?" Trent intervened.

"Sure...go ahead," the officer relented.

"Why are you pushing so hard for me to get into your program? Is it because you have the hots for my mother? Because that's not going to work. If you want to ask her to go out with you, do it, but don't use me as an excuse to try to go out with her."

Officer Hadley's face flamed up. Lois could see the embarrassment and the resentment in his eyes. Trent had been right. That's what this was about. Hadley didn't give a damn if Trent joined his program or not; he just wanted more access to Lois. *What a jerk!*

"My son is right, isn't he? You really don't care if he joins or not. You have your own agenda. How dare you? Officer Hadley, my son means everything to me. I would do anything for him….*for him*, Officer Hadley. You asked me to go out with you and I said no. Do you know why I said no? Because I don't want to go out with you or anybody else! But I surely would never go out with a man who attempted to use my son as a pawn to get what he wants. I think you should leave….now." She stood up and Hadley followed suit. He quietly left without a word. When Lois heard the front door close she sank down onto the chair again and rubbed her temples.

"Way to go, Mom! High five!" Trent's face was split into a big grin. Lois high-fived him and began to laugh. Before long both of them were laughing and holding their sides. Between rounds of laughter, Trent eked out, "I knew he hit on you."

Lois didn't deny it.

Chapter 15

Lois managed to get the invoice for damages paid by the time school ended for the year. Trent was now out of middle school, and after the summer vacation, he would start into his first year of high school. *High school! Where did the years go? You would be proud of him, Jonathan—wherever you are.*

It was almost the end of June. Lois had done quite well in underwriting policies for the past year, and her income had increased to the point where she could just about meet all the household expenses and even give Trent a little something upon occasion. At quitting time, on Friday the week before the Fourth of July Holiday, her boss walked by her desk and handed her an envelope.

"What is this?" She asked.

"Open it."

She opened the envelope and found a check written in her name for one thousand dollars! "What is this for?" She seemed totally perplexed.

"Bonus money. You've done well. Keep up the good work and there will be more of these." The boss smiled and winked at her and then left for the day.

She gathered her things and left shortly before four o'clock so she could deposit the check into the bank. What a surprise! What should she do with the extra money? And then it hit her. She knew what she was going to do. She hurried home, hoping Trent would be there. He wasn't, but he came in shortly after she entered the house.

"Hi, kiddo....where were you?"

"Up at Jason's. We were shooting hoops."

"That's nice. Hey....I want to talk to you. I have some good news."

"You found my dad?"

"No," Lois answered, letting her heart sink a little. "I got a bonus from work and I was wondering if you would like to go to the shore for a couple of days over the Fourth of July weekend."

"That would be great! Could Jason go with us?"

"Let me think about that while you call and order

us a pizza and a couple of salads for dinner." She mulled it over in her mind. She really didn't care for Jason, but he was Trent's friend. Maybe it would be good for both boys to take a little trip out of town. She was sure Trent would have a better time having a friend there instead of just hanging around with his mother. She would get some down time that way, too.

"Pizza's ordered. They said forty minutes." Trent piped up from the kitchen. Lois came out of her room, shoeless, wearing a pair of shorts and a tank top.

"Good. Okay....I thought about it. If Jason's mother will let him go, he can go with us. I'll call her right now if you'd like."

Lois made the call and Rita Blake seemed all too happy to get rid of her son that weekend. So be it. Lois would have both boys for the extended weekend. Although he tried to hide it, she could see that Trent was excited at the prospect of going on a vacation. She just wondered how she was going to manage the sleeping arrangements.

She needn't have worried. She lucked out when she called a summer rental agent in the Virginia Beach area. The agency had had a cancellation just that day and there was a small three-room cottage available for the entire week-end! The rental agent told her it was just five cottages away from the sandy beach and she could have it for the weekend for a mere five hundred dollars, since the original renter forfeited his deposit. The place had two bedrooms and an open living room-kitchen area. There were small appliances there for convenience. The agent said the place was small but clean, comfortable, and reasonable. Lois was ecstatic. She reached into her purse and pulled out her credit card, which she had only used one other time. She gave the agent the numbers and the expiration date, and waited while he ran the card.

"Okay, Miss Watkins, You're all set. Let me give you directions to our office and you can pick up the key on Friday night. We're here until nine o'clock. Will you be here by then?"

"Yes, we will. Is there some sort of confirmation I'll need to identify my reservation?"

"Oh, yes….one moment, please." He came back on the line with a confirmation for her and she wrote it down. She hung up and turned to Trent.

"Okay….we have a place!" She was grinning and so was he.

While they were eating the newly arrived pizza, they made a list of what they would need for their weekend. Trent needed new swim trunks—Lois hoped her swimsuit still fit. A spending budget was developed, allotting for meals, entertainment, and other incidentals. Their planning was interrupted twice by

Jason who was just as excited as Trent. Each time his calls were about what to bring with him.

"It sounds to me like he's packing already," Lois laughed.

"Yeah, he probably is. Jason has never been out of town. At least we went to the shore that one time. And then to the lake with…" Trent stopped and looked the other way.

"Well, if you stay out of trouble from now on, we should be able to take a couple of trips now and then."

"What about the car, Mom? Will it make it there with no problems?"

"Already have that covered. Since Aunt Jackie has plans that don't include her car, she's lending it to us."

"Cool! Her car is really cool!"

"Yeah, it is," Lois sighed and smiled, thinking about her friend's new Saturn SUV she had just purchased. It was small but roomy inside. Trent loved its black exterior and contrasting pale gray interior.

For the first time since it was over between her and Garrett, Lois had something to look forward to. She was glad she decided to do this, and she silently thanked her boss for making it possible.

Carole McKee

Chapter 16

Lois found the rental agency without any problem. She pulled into a space just left of the agency and ran in to sign the rental agreement and pick up the key. Trent and Jason waited in the car.

"This is so cool, Trent. We can do a lot of shit down here." Jason spoke through his large grin.

"Yeah, I know. Sometimes my mother is pretty cool. I just wish I could meet my dad. My mom says I look just like him, only smaller and thinner."

"Hey, wouldn't it be cool if we ran into him down here?"

"Nah. My mom says he's from Pennsylvania."

"So? People from Pennsylvania come here, too. Did you ever see a picture of him?"

"Yeah, my mom has one."

"So you would know him if you saw him, right?"

"I guess," he responded with a shrug.

Inside the rental agency, Lois signed the agreement, showed her credit card, and was handed the key.

"Okay, Lois....is it okay if I call you Lois?"

"Yes, of course," Lois answered and nodded.

"We're here all weekend if you need anything. The cottage is down this road, on the left. It's yellow with white shutters, just five away from the beach. Here is a map of the area, a merchant's map of the boardwalk, and some complimentary coupons for a couple of the vendors, a listing of attractions, and also the schedule of events for this weekend. Have fun, be safe, and treat the cottage as though it were your own. You can drop the key through the mail slot when you leave if we're not here then. Oh, and take my card. This is my direct cell phone line right here." He pointed with his index finger at the number on the bottom of the card.

Lois smiled and thanked him, and ran back to the car. "Okay, let's find this place," she said to the boys. She drove slowly down the road, going even slower over the speed bumps. She spotted the cottage and pulled up in front of it. "Here we are," she announced, and shut the car off.

After trying the key in the door, making sure it fit, they ran back to the car to unload. The boys grabbed the duffel bags and luggage and Lois picked up the bags of food she had purchased at the local grocery store close to home. The boys made a second trip to the car to get the bedding and towels they were required to bring. Lois was glad she brought hotdogs and marshmallows when she spied the charcoal grill in front of the cottage. That would cut down on some of the expenses.

"Okay, guys….I'll make up the beds…you empty out the grocery bags and put them away. Trent, see if that little refrigerator is plugged in. Make sure it's on."

Lois had the beds ready in no time, even before the boys had the food put away. She finished the job for them. "Now what? Want to check out the beach? Or the boardwalk?"

"Yeah! The boardwalk! That should be fun. Remember when we were here with Aunt Jackie, Mom?"

"I do, Trent. That was quite a few years ago. I'm sure things have changed since then. Here's some money, guys. Twenty dollars for each of you. That way you won't have to keep asking for money."

"Wow....cool!" Both boys responded, barely containing their excitement.

They found the boardwalk without any effort and began the stroll along past merchants and vendors. The boys were drawn like magnets to an arcade where there were games, both electronic and the old-fashioned pinball variety. Along the left wall there was skeet-ball. Lois remembered how much fun she had playing skeet-ball with Jonathan at the carnival. She got a roll of quarters and began rolling the balls as soon as an alley opened. She played until her quarters ran out and then went to cash in her tickets for a prize. Trent and Jason were still occupied with the electronic game in which they were battling each other, so Lois stepped outside of the arcade to find a place for dinner. A sign boasting of the best burgers on the boardwalk was posted in the window right next door. Perfect.

She closed in on the boys just as they finished the game and intercepted the hand that was about to place more money into the coin slot. "Let's eat. You can come back, but I am starving."

"Yeah, I'm kind of hungry, too," Trent conceded. "But we can come back to this place?"

"Of course. How about the place next door for food? They say they have the best burgers on the boardwalk..." she tempted.

"Sounds great, Mom. I'm ready."

Lois had no idea if the burgers were the best on the boardwalk, but she was certain that they were the best she had ever tasted. They each ordered the double cheeseburger platter and all three of them devoured even the last crumb on their plates. When she was sated and full, Lois opened her purse and pulled out the coupons that the rental agent had given her.

"Oh look...we have a coupon for donuts from the donut shop...and here's one for pizza.....and yes...one for this place. Oh, and look...we have five dollar off coupons for the amusement park right behind this boardwalk."

"Wow...cool...this is going to be a great weekend, huh, Mom?"

"I'm hoping, Trent. I'm looking forward to the beach tomorrow. After all this food, though....I don't know. I might look like a beached whale in my black and white swimsuit. I know I plan on taking up jogging when we get back home."

"You look great, Mrs. Watkins," Jason piped up. "More like a mermaid than a beached whale."

"Why Jason....flattery doesn't count when it's your friend's mother," Lois laughed.

Carole McKee

Chapter 17

Lois felt quite rested after a good night's sleep. She arose early and was surprised to discover that the boys were not in the cottage. She quickly threw on a robe and walked outside to see if she could see them anywhere. A wave of relief washed over her when she spotted them walking from the sand back to the cottage.

"What were you doing?" She asked when they got within earshot.

"Just checking out the beach. Here….I brought you this." Trent extended his hand holding a seashell and Lois reached for it.

"What a lovely pink seashell. Thank you, Honey. Want to go get those donuts this morning? You and Jason can go get them while I make up the beds." *And get to the shower first.*

"Okay!"

Lois handed him the coupon and a five dollar bill, and the boys took off immediately toward the boardwalk. "Get them and come right back!" She shouted after them.

Quickly, she ran in and took her shower in the tiny bathroom, dressed, and made the beds. She was about to make coffee when she realized there was no coffee maker. She sighed her disappointment but shrugged it off, deciding that it would probably be better for her if she gave up the coffee for the weekend anyway. Just as she had herself convinced it was for the best, someone knocked on her door. It was the rental agent. He had introduced himself as Tom Moore when she picked up the key the day before.

"Hi, Lois....I brought you a cup of coffee. I realized late last night that this cottage didn't have a coffee maker so I brought that, too. The one that was in here quit working, so I removed it last week. Here is the replacement for it. Since I didn't have it here by the time you arrived, I brought you coffee. There's cream and sugar in the bag."

"Well, thank you, Mr. Moore. I just about had myself convinced that I didn't need the coffee for the weekend. I'm glad you brought me to my senses," she joked, "And put me out of misery, I might add." She reached for the coffee, added the cream she found in the bag, and watched as he set up the new coffee maker. He washed out the pot and put the packet of coffee grounds that came with the appliance inside, filled the carafe with water, and flipped the switch to 'on.'

"So what did you do last night? You have a couple of kids with you, right?"

"Yes...my son, Trent and his friend Jason. They just left to go pick up donuts. We went to the boardwalk, and of course, the boys found the arcade, then we ate at that burger place. They went back to the arcade and I walked around, just looking." Lois could hear the boys talking and laughing as they came close to the cottage. "I can hear them coming now. Would you like to stay and have a cup of coffee and a donut?"

"Sure, I would love to. It's only nine. We don't open the office for another hour." He cocked his head toward the door and then stepped up to open it. He held the door as the boys piled in with two boxes of donuts.

"How many did you get?" Lois squealed in surprise when they set two boxes of donuts down.

"Two dozen. That's what the coupon was for. All we had to pay was three dollars. Who's this guy?" Trent asked, nodding his head toward Tom.

"This is Mr. Moore. He's the rental agent who we rented this place from. He brought me a coffee pot."

"Good...now you won't get crabby," he teased.

"Trent...I do *not* get crabby." Lois laughed. "Mr. Moore, this is my son Trent and his friend, Jason."

"Hi guys....what do you think of the place so far? I'm sure there are a lot of things you haven't seen yet."

"It's really cool here. Do you live here all year?"

"Well, not far from here. I like to come down to the beach when all the tourist traffic is gone. Late fall is my favorite time."

"I guess you have the beach to yourself then...right?"

"Yeah, pretty much. So what do you have planned today?"

"Mom wants to be on the beach, and then tonight we're going to the amusement park. Right, Mom?"

"If that's what you want to do, Honey."

"Can we go back to the arcade for awhile today? While you're getting sunburned on the beach?"

"Oh...I suppose. They love that arcade." Lois smiled at the rental agent as she opened the donut boxes and folded the flaps and the lids back. "Please sit down.

Trent and Jason, do you want some orange juice?" She added as she got the Styrofoam cups out of the cupboard. When the orange juice was poured and the coffee was ready they all sat down to eat the donuts.

Trent noticed that the rental agent couldn't keep his eyes off of his mother. He warily studied the man, watching for a sign of something—he wasn't sure what. At least the guy didn't pretend to be interested in him. He hated that. Like that cop...acting like he was trying to do something nice for the son, when all he wanted was to get in good with the son's mother.

"Do you have a wife?" Trent blurted out, surprising everyone at the table, including himself.

"Trent! That's none of your business!" Lois scolded.

"That's all right, Lois. No, Trent, I don't. Why do you ask?"

Trent shrugged. "Just wondering," he mumbled.

"I'm sorry, Mr. Moore..."

"Tom."

"Tom. I'm sorry for my son's impertinent question."

"That's okay. I'm a widower. My wife died about seven years ago. We were only married a short time when she got sick."

"Oh....I'm so sorry. You must miss her terribly."

"Well, yes...but it has been seven years. You never get over it, but it does get easier. We had been married for only a year and a half when she began to have symptoms. She put up a hell of a fight, but in the end she lost her battle with leukemia. How about you? Are you married, divorced, widowed?"

"No...none of the above. It's just me and Trent."

"That can't be easy."

"Sometimes it isn't," she admitted and then smiled, glad that that particular line of questioning ended.

After sharing a couple of donuts and another cup of coffee, Tom Moore went to the rental office. Lois, Trent and Jason got ready to head to the beach.

"Mom, I think that guy likes you," Trent informed her as they were walking toward the sand.

"Who? What guy?"

"Mr. Moore. He likes you."

"Well, of course he does. I just paid him five hundred dollars. The people who cancelled lost what they had paid for the cottage, so he made a nice little profit from me. So of course he likes me," she assured him, grinning.

"I think he likes you because of other reasons."

"What reasons would that be?" She raised her left eyebrow as she stared at him.

"I don't know. Because he thinks you're pretty, maybe? Maybe he wants to go out with you. I don't know."

Lois ruffled his already too-long hair. "Nothing to worry about, Trent. He's just being nice."

"I'm *not* worried," Trent assured her.

Carole McKee

Chapter 18

The entrance to the amusement park was in plain sight. After a day on the beach and then a stop at Boardwalk Pizzeria for a late lunch, they went back to the cottage, showered, and then started walking to the amusement park. It was just after six when they saw the entrance to the park. The rides were just starting up after being closed all day while the beachgoers enjoyed the beach and the boardwalk. Just as they were about to enter through the amusement park gates, the boys spotted Tom Moore, standing just outside the gate eating an ice cream cone.

"Hi, Mr. Moore," they called.

He walked toward them, grinning. "Well, hi there. How was the beach?" He asked the boys while he fervently studied Lois.

"It was great! Are you going into the park?" Trent asked him.

"I think so. I like the coaster, so I usually look for a partner to ride with me. I enjoy amusement parks a lot." *Like Jonathan, Lois remembered.*

"We want to go on it. Maybe you could ride with my mom, 'cause me and Jason are going to ride in the first car." *Is the darling boy match-making?*

"Well, I'd be delighted, if it's okay with *you*, Lois."

"Go ahead, Mom. That way me and Jason can pick up girls."

"WHAT?" Lois's head spun around as she gasped in shock. *Oh no! When did this start? Girls? Already? Don't they still have cooties or something?*

"Aren't you a little young for that?" She asked in between her silent prayer.

"Mom...I'm thirteen. I like girls. It's okay if I do, isn't it?"

Lois was visibly shaken. Her son was already interested in girls? It was going to be time for *The Talk.* Oh, how she wished she had a brother. *Or a husband.* She glanced at Tom and saw that he was trying to hide a grin by holding his hand over his mouth. Thankfully, he saved the moment.

"Okay...I'll tell you what. I'll ride the rides with your mother, but we meet somewhere every hour. Is that okay with you, Lois?"

Lois knew she had to answer the question, but she was still trying to get the wads of cotton out of her mouth and throat. Her body felt numb with shock. When did Trent become interested in the opposite sex? *Come on, Lois—what did you expect? It had to happen eventually. Eventually, yes--but right now? We're on vacation!*

"Come on, Mom! You should have some fun."

"Yeah, Lois...if your son wants to act like a grown-up you can act like a kid again. So come on...let's have fun."

Slowly, Lois was recovering from the shock. "I....I guess it'll be okay. I'm sorry....but that was quite a shock to me. I'm a mother. My son shouldn't grow up on me like that." She laughed lightly, trying to lift the protective blanket of fog that had settled over her— compliments of the part of her brain that controlled her emotions. "Where should we meet?"

"How about right there by the ice cream stand? Every hour you guys have to show up, or we call the park police. Fair enough?"

The boys agreed and Lois handed them the string bracelets they had to put on their wrists so they could gain passage to all rides in the park. They shot off like launched rockets, leaving behind a confused woman drowning in awkwardness. "Wow," was all she could say at the moment of their departure. Tom cleared his throat.

"I don't have any kids, so I'm not an expert, but isn't this some kind of a milestone in your relationship?"

Lois tilted her head to the side and stared up at Tom, her eyes shimmering bright green. "Yes...I guess it is," she agreed.

"Come on....let's get in line for the roller coaster."

Almost reluctantly, Lois followed Tom to the coaster line. As they moved forward, she felt as though she was missing an arm. *Get used to it, Lois. He's growing up.* They joined the line behind others and waited for it to move forward.

"So I take it you and Trent's father never married." The statement was almost, but not quite a question.

"No, we didn't...and thank you for not pursuing that earlier today. Trent's been giving me a little grief on the matter. I don't know where his father is. He never knew about Trent and he still doesn't."

"You never tried to get in touch with him?"

"Yeah, a couple of times, but he never responded. The letters weren't returned so I guess he got them. I never mentioned the baby when I wrote. I didn't want him to think that I was begging for anything, I guess."

As they talked, the line was moving forward and they were moving with it. Before they knew it, they were in a coaster car and ready for take-off.

The evening was fun for Lois, and apparently for Trent and Jason, too. As agreed, the boys met them back at the ice cream stand every hour—one time showing up with two skinny little girls who were all starry-eyed over them. Trent sidled up to his mother and whispered a plea for a few dollars that time. She quietly and subtly handed him two tens, mentally sighing. As she and Tom were headed toward the tilt-a-whirl, Tom confessed to her that he had given the boys a couple of bucks to buy the girls a coke or an ice cream. Lois was fuming over that. So the boys had gotten more than the ten each she had given them. The little con artists! She would deal with them later.

The park stayed open until one, but it was close to midnight and Lois had had it. She was ready to get back to the cottage and enter the land of slumber. While they were waiting for Trent and Jason to appear on the hour, Tom bought them a cup of coffee.

"It's decaf, so I hope that's okay."

"It's fine….thank you, Tom. I had fun tonight."

"Yeah, I did, too. I think the boys had fun."

"Yeah…how about those girls? They looked like

Trent and Jason were the best things to come along since Santa Claus." Lois laughed.

"Well, those two are going to be real heart-breakers. Good-looking boys...especially Trent. Those eyes are pretty unusual. Yours are green."

"Yes, he has his father's eyes," Lois told him.

"I see them coming....so before they get here, I have to ask. Can I see you again?"

Before Lois could answer both boys were standing in front of her, groaning because she was making them leave the park.

Chapter 19

Lois was sound asleep and into a dream. She was dreaming that someone was hammering on the roof of the cottage next door. It continued non-stop and was becoming annoying. She rolled over, bringing her to the surface of her fitful sleep. The hammering didn't stop. She was all the way awake now. It wasn't hammering; someone was knocking at the door. Grabbing a robe, she ran to the door and turned on the outside light. Lois sensed trouble when she saw two men and a woman standing at the door. She knew she had locked the screen door, so she opened the inside door a few inches.

"Yes?" She spoke warily.

"Do you have two sons?"

"No, I have a son, but he's here with a friend. Why?"

"Ma'am, can you check to see if they are here? Please."

Lois briskly walked the short distance between the door and the boys' room, and peered into it. She couldn't detect the sleeping forms of the boys so she snapped on the light. They weren't there! Lois felt the bile rising up into her throat as her heart began to palpitate. Her hands were shaking as the panic was about to take over. Where had they gone, and why were these people at the door asking about them? She had to find out, so she ran back to the door.

"Uh….they're not in bed. I…I don't know where they are. Oh my God…where would they have gone? And why are you here asking about them?"

"May we come in?" The tallest of the men asked her. She opened the door wider and stood aside letting the three of them pass through.

"I'm John Peters and this is my wife, Miriam. This is my brother, Joe," he added, indicating the other man. "We're up here from Raleigh just taking a little vacation. Our daughters are missing." An image of the two skinny girls flashed through Lois's mind. "Well, anyway….to make a long story short, our daughters were with your two boys at the amusement park last night. We think they all may have snuck out together."

Lois wasn't sure whether she should feel relieved or angry. She settled for both. *Already sneaking out with girls? Growing up is one thing, but sneaking out in the middle of the night to meet girls? Not acceptable!*

"We have the police looking for them now." *The police!*

Lois wrapped her arms around her waist just to fend off the shivers that were trying to overcome her. "How did you know to come here?" She asked.

"My son said he saw where you were staying when he was walking around on the trails. He had seen the girls with your son and the other boy at the amusement park."

Lois nodded. It was the only function she was able to manage at that moment, but she put her mind in gear within a few seconds. Freezing up now was not going to help matters. She offered to make coffee for everyone, but they declined; as they sat in near silence.

"You must be a single parent," the woman introduced as Miriam concluded.

"Yes, I am." Lois responded.

"Well, that explains it," John Peters snorted. "You don't have control over your son, do you?"

Lois's blood began to boil. She wasn't going to take that from him. "Now just a minute...your daughter is out there somewhere, too. There are two of you….double the parentage…and the two of you obviously don't have any more control over your child than I have over mine. Don't blame it on my being a single parent. These things happen. And before you ask…this is the first time it has ever happened with my son. Hopefully it will be the last, since he will be grounded until he is eighteen after this." Her verbal stance was met with silence until Joe Peters cleared his throat.

"We apologize. We didn't mean to imply that this is your fault, or even your son's fault. All four kids are at fault. We're just all getting a little edgy." John Peters tapped his fingers on his knees as he spoke. "I think I could use a cup of that coffee if you're still offering."

Lois readied the coffee maker and flipped the switch to on. She reached into the cupboard and brought out cups before she sat down again. She had to get right back up to answer another knock at the door. Joe's wife was out of breath like she had run all the way from the closest town.

"The police have all four of them right now. They're on their way here," she informed them, just as headlights approached the cottage.

Lois watched as four police officers herded the four youths out of the two police cars and into the small cottage. All four of them looked frightened. *Good.* Not uttering a word, Lois folded her arms over her chest and stared straight into Trent's soul and watched him cowl under her scrutiny. Everybody seemed to be talking at once. The girls were crying and the mothers were chastising. The fathers were making small idle threats to the two boys. The officer in charge asked for quiet, and then began to speak.

"Okay.....we found all four of them just under the pier. All four were smoking cigarettes and these two young ladies were nude from the waist up."

Lois's gasp was muffled by the sound of four other gasps. The girls averted their eyes to the floor, while Jason and Trent visually connected, both wearing a smirk. Lois was one step from slapping that smirk off both of their faces. The police passed out citations to the parents, and of course Lois got two, for having two boys. Since it was a holiday weekend, the police fined them each twenty-five dollars and told all four kids that they better not be caught in that situation again. The cottage was exceptionally quiet when the police and the two sets of parents finally left. Lois turned on Trent, her face a mask of rage.

"What were you thinking? I want an explanation, and I want it now! Why were those girls undressed? And where...and when did you start smoking? Begin talking *now*!"

"It was their idea to sneak out! They told us to meet them! And it was their idea to take their clothes off, I swear! They asked us if we wanted to see their boobs….and….and…we said….sure! So they did it."

"And the smoking?" Lois dismissed their story about the girls. *Fat chance that that was true! Ha!*

"We…we just tried it….that's all." Trent hung his head in remorse.

"And…?"

"I won't do it again, Mom….honest."

Lois sent both boys to bed, with the intent that the discussion would continue in the morning. She knew she had to calm down a little in order to be rational, but this conversation was far from over.

Chapter 20

Bright sunshine poured through the small cottage, targeting Lois's face, forcing her to get up off the small sofa and start a pot of coffee. Her head was pounding. She had elected to sleep on the lumpy sofa in order to assure herself that the boys would not go back out after she fell asleep, and this morning her bones were protesting her decision. While the coffee was dripping down into the carafe, she hurried into the bathroom, took a quick shower, and returned to the kitchen to freshly brewed coffee. What was she going to do about the boys' actions last night? She knew they were not going to the arcade, and that was a punishment in itself, and for the rest of the weekend they were not going to be allowed to go anywhere unless she went with them. Now *that* was real punishment for thirteen year old boys! Of course, she was going to have to tell Jason's mother about what happened, but somehow she didn't believe the woman would even care.

Lois's brain was scrambled. All this was happening too fast. Trent picking up girls. Trent sneaking out to meet girls. Trent smoking cigarettes. What would it be next? She couldn't allow herself to lose control. She would lose Trent forever if she did.

Her thoughts were interrupted by a squeak in the floorboards. Trent and Jason stood in front of the table looking sheepish and just cute as hell. She hardened her melting heart and scowled at them.

"So....what do you have to say for yourselves?"

"I guess you're still really mad....right, Mrs. Watkins?" Jason didn't look as apprehensive as Trent.

"Yes...I am still really angry. Trent, you and I have had this discussion about choices. Choices bring consequences. Bad choices...bad consequences....good choices...well, you know what I'm talking about. Right?" Trent nodded. "So what would possess the two of you to sneak out of here and go meet those two girls? You know I wouldn't have allowed it. That's why you had to sneak. So why did you do it?"

"Those girls said they did it all the time."

"And that makes it right?" Lois challenged.

'No....we just didn't want to look like....some kind of creepy nerds"

"Well, guess what. Now you're going to look like

creepy nerds....because you aren't going anywhere I'm not going. What do you want for breakfast?"

Lois and the boys spent a couple of hours at the beach collecting seashells, and then strolled on the boardwalk for another couple of hours.

"Let's get something for Aunt Jackie....and Jason's mother." Lois suggested.   Jason found an ashtray that said 'Virginia Beach' for his mother. The bottom of the ashtray was weighted with sand and tiny shells. *Well, she was a smoker, after all.* Trent looked for the perfect gift for Jackie but wasn't having much luck. Finally he decided on a turquoise tee-shirt with the Virginia Beach logo across the front of it. He felt it was unique because the hem of the shirt was purposely frayed to look tattered. Jackie would love it, Lois was sure. They headed back to the cottage around three. All three of them were feeling the effect of the sun's rays, even though they had worn sunscreen.

"We're going to cook on the grill tonight. I saw a general store up next to the rental office, and I'll bet they carry charcoal and lighter fluid. Let's see, we need those two items, and maybe some potatoes or potato salad. We have marshmallows, so we don't really need a dessert."

"We'll walk up there for you." Trent volunteered.

"Oh, of course you will. You're grounded."

"We'll come right back....we promise."

"And I should believe you, why?"

"Aw, Mom....we will....we promise."

"Okay," Lois relented. "Let me write down what you have to get." She made a quick list and handed Trent some money and watched them walk up toward the general store.

Trent and Jason entered the store and quickly grabbed all the items on the list. They had to move fast, since they had taken a longer detour to get there. Jason wanted to stop and smoke a cigarette, and of course, Trent joined him. They purchased a pack of gum to hide the smell from Lois.

"I guess we're still in trouble with your mom."

"Yeah, it looks that way. Wouldn't your mom be pissed?"

"Nah...she'd just say I was an asshole like my father."

Trent stared at Jason and then looked away. *His* mom never said anything bad about *his* father. That was one of the reasons Trent wanted to meet him so badly.

"We aren't going to have any more fun this weekend unless we can soften her up." Trent was holding the door for Jason since he had the bag of charcoal. Just as he shut the door behind Jason, Trent glanced over at the rental office and saw Tom Moore just getting out of his car. "I got an idea. Hey, Mr. Moore!" Trent called, as he trotted toward him.

"Hi...hey, we're cooking on the grill tonight. Want to come down for hotdogs, potato salad, and marshmallows?"

"Well, thank you for the invite. Did your mother tell you to invite me?"

"No....not exactly...but she would love to have you come. She likes you, I think. She says you're nice."

"Are you sure she wouldn't mind?"

"No...she wouldn't. Can you be there at five-thirty?"

"Sure...as long as you're sure it's okay."

"It is....see you then." Trent looked at Jason with a smirk on his face as they walked away toward the cottages. "Mission accomplished," he grinned.

Lois heard the boys coming, so she pulled the charcoal grill out away from the cottage and waited. She was impressed that they had gotten everything on her list, but not impressed when they told her they invited Tom Moore.

"Now why would you do that? How could you invite him without checking with me first?" She stood with her hand on her hip, glaring at Trent and Jason,

"You said he was nice. We just thought you would like it if he came down and ate dinner with us."

"And of course, I'd remove you from being grounded...."

"No...we didn't think that....honest."

Lois sighed and shook her head as she grabbed the bag of charcoal and dumped it in the grill, and then poured the lighter fluid on top. She struck a match and threw it into the mix, backing up as the flames shot straight up. Just as the coals were hot enough to put the hotdogs on, Tom Moore pulled up in his car and parked alongside of the SUV. Smiling, he got out of the car holding a bag in his hand. "I bring contributions," he joked.

"Hi....and what did you bring?"

Tom handed her the bag and she peered inside at the most delicious looking cake and a container of pasta salad.

"Wow! That cake looks wonderful!"

"Yeah, it's called a torte cake. I hope you don't mind me coming. The boys assured me that you would be happy to have me for dinner."

Lois smiled at him. He was really a very nice man, and no, she didn't mind him coming to dinner. Looking around, she noticed the boys had conveniently disappeared into the cottage. "I'll let you in on a little secret. They got into trouble last night and they are grounded. Inviting you is a ploy to lighten their punishment." She elaborated on what had happened the night before, and Tom listened intently. When she finished the tale, he spoke after a moment of silence.

"I think you should know that those two little girls have done that before. Their parents come here every year, and those two have been sneaking out and doing things with boys since they were eleven. Believe me, your two boys are the innocents here."

Hearing that was a great relief to Lois, but she was sure that there would be more issues like that coming in the future, and the future was right around the corner.

Chapter 21

Aside from the one night, the weekend had been relaxing, fun, and stress-free, Lois silently noted as she was driving toward their home. The boys had a good time, she was sure. She laughed to herself when she thought about how they tried to set her up with Tom Moore. Did they think she was born yesterday? Tom had, however, asked if she would mind if he came to see her once in awhile—maybe have dinner. She had agreed to that because he *was* a nice man and apparently very lonely. She felt no sparks there, but he was easy company. If he should show up on her doorstep she would be fine with it. As she drove she realized that she had almost completely stopped playing the 'what if' game and directing and producing the mind movies. Trent was blasting an FM radio station on the car radio, and she could see him keeping time to the music from the rear view mirror. She sighed. She loved him so much—so much that she was putting all of her hopes and dreams on the back burner. No, not on the back burner—locked in a trunk in some dark attic—and she lost the key. *Jonathan. What was his life like? Did he have other kids? A wife? Money in the bank? A nice home? Must be nice, if you do have all this, Jonathan. I could use a little help from you once in awhile.* She knew she was thinking unfairly, since she hadn't had the guts to tell him that she had gotten pregnant when she wrote to him. Maybe he would have gotten in touch with her.

Lois slowed down and pulled up in front of Jason's house. She helped him untangle his belongings from the rest of the things in the car, and walked up the front steps with him. She fully intended to tell his mother about the incident and the citation she had to pay.

"Thank you for taking me, Mrs. Watkins. I had a great time. Sorry about the thing with the girls. I mean…I'm *really* sorry about that." Lois softened a little. "I don't think my mom's at home. If you wanted to see her, she may be at the bar on the corner. She goes there sometimes on a Sunday night. She walks so she doesn't get caught drinking and driving." *How thoughtful and considerate of the rest of the world.*

Lois' intentions melted away, and she just stood and watched until Jason was inside and a light came on. That kid had enough on his plate, just maintaining a normal life of school and social activities alone.

She hopped back in the car and drove home. While

she and Trent were unloading the car, Jackie pulled up.

"Aunt Jackie! I got you something!" Trent shouted immediately.

"Hi there! How was the weekend?"

"Great," both of the Watkins answered in unison.

"Want to go watch fireworks?"

They both eagerly accepted her invitation and all three jumped into the SUV, Jackie behind the wheel this time. On the way to the park hosting the fireworks, Jackie told them about her weekend and then listened to the details of theirs. She was in shock over the incident with the girls, she said. And Trent smoking? That was even more of a shock. She made up her mind to have a private talk with him as soon as possible.

After a marvelous fireworks display, they went back to the house and finished off the delicious torte cake Tom had brought to the cookout. Lois made a pot of coffee and she and Jackie chatted, just enjoying each other's companionship. Trent had gone to his room and they could hear the music blasting.

"When did he become a teenager?" Jackie laughed.

"Oh God...I'm not sure, Jackie. We left out the part about when the cops found the kids, the girls were nude from the waist up."

Jackie's eyes widened. "No way!" She contradicted.

Lois nodded. "Yes, way."

"Wow! Now tell me about Tom."

"Oh...there's not really much to tell. He was very nice. We had fun on the amusement rides. He was nice to talk to. No spark, no sizzle, nothing. It was just nice to talk to a male who had already been through puberty," Lois laughed, and so did Jackie.

Shortly after that, Trent came out to say goodnight.

"Hey, Trent....I'm off work for the next couple of days. How about we do something tomorrow?"

"Like what?" He asked.

"How about I pick you up and we do lunch and then go ride some go-carts? How does that sound?"

"Cool, Aunt Jackie! That sounds great!"

"Okay with you, Lois?"

Lois nodded her approval, knowing that she was breaking the grounding rule. Trent went into his room and shut the door.

"We're going to have a talk about cigarettes tomorrow," Jackie informed Lois. "The other talk is up to you."

Lois pulled her lips into a grimace and nodded in agreement. "That talk has to be soon...too soon."

"Has he mentioned his father lately?"

"Yes...more than usual. I think it's because his friend Jason has contact with his own father...although apparently he isn't much of a father. It seems both of Jason's parents lack in the supervision and attention areas."

"I guess Trent doesn't realize how lucky he is that he has you for a single parent. At least there is love and caring along with supervision. He will realize that when he's older."

"Yeah, if he gets much older. Sometimes I'm close to taking him out of this world," she joked.

Jackie laughed. "I know it can't be easy, but basically, Trent's a good kid. He's just all boy. And you love him."

"With all my heart," Lois smiled.

Carole McKee

Chapter 22

Lois no longer drove Trent to and from school. He was now in the tenth grade and he preferred to walk to school with friends or just by himself. At fifteen, he had outgrown his mother's protection and companionship. Friday and Saturday nights found Lois alone and waiting for Trent to come home. He had an eleven o'clock curfew and so far he had been punctual, even though he tried to convince her to stretch the time on several occasions. She assured him that when he was sixteen she would give him more leeway, but not until then.

Trent, Jason, and Kevin, a newfound friend had become inseparable, and many weekend nights, Lois had all three boys overnight, playing the X-Box Lois bought for Trent on his fifteenth birthday. She had been getting bonus money regularly since the first one was handed to her almost two years prior to this last one. Each of them was for more than a thousand dollars and she managed to give Trent something nice from each of them. The balance went into his college fund, which had grown considerably in the past two years.

The X-Box was a good investment since she had Trent—and Trent's friends—at her place, rather than at Jason's or Kevin's. She didn't like Trent going to Jason's because of all the cigarette smoking, drinking, and from what she had heard, a parade of men going through the door. She knew very little about Kevin's family, and would not allow Trent to stay at his place until she met the parents, much to Trent's indignation.

Tonight all three boys were staying at her house. They were out and about somewhere but should be home at the promised and enforced curfew. It had just begun to get dark when someone knocked on the door. *Tom!*

"Hi, Lois….I hope I'm not interrupting anything. I mean, sorry to barge in on you but I happened to have a reason to be in Richmond so I thought I would look you up. I hope you don't mind." Tom had called her a couple of times, but this was his first visit.

"Tom….not at all….please, come in." Lois smiled, genuinely glad to see him.

"Where's Trent?" He asked her.

"Oh, out somewhere with his friends."

"Yeah, I guess he'd be….what…fifteen now?"

"Yes, he is….and too big for his britches sometimes," she laughed. "Can I make you some coffee?"

"That would be wonderful, since I brought this good-looking cake with me."

Lois smiled and told him to sit down while she made the coffee. He had no idea how welcome his visit was. She had very little adult companionship, especially since her best friend, Jackie had suddenly fallen in love with the new pharmacist at Walgreen's. They had been dating for the past six months and it appeared to be getting serious. She was happy for Jackie but losing the close friendship was hard on her.

"Sorry I haven't been in touch more," Tom apologized over a cup of hot coffee and a piece of the delicious caramel, chocolate cake he brought. "I wanted to, but then I was working so hard all summer and actually into October these last couple of years….and then I took on more realty property to rent out and supervise. So I have been swamped with work. I had to come into Richmond today to meet with an advertising agency….and here I am."

"Well, I'm glad you stopped," Lois assured him. "I was just sitting here reading. Trent and his friends are due here at eleven. All three boys will be spending the night."

"How did you manage that?"

"X-Box," she laughed.

"So how has it been going? Are you used to Trent's elderly ways yet?"

She burst out laughing, and it felt good. She hadn't laughed like that in years. *Elderly ways...that was funny.* "Yes....and no," she admitted. "He's all I have. Seeing him grow up is rewarding, if not challenging, but it's also frightening for me. What if he grows up and leaves? Oh, I know he's going to....eventually...but being without him..."

"Have you thought about meeting someone and maybe having a relationship?"

She chuckled. "Years ago....yes....but I haven't thought about it in quite awhile."

"Lois...you forgot how to dream....didn't you?"

"I guess I did."

"I know how that is. When my wife died, I didn't dream any more. I still don't. When we met at the beach I felt that you were someone I could talk to, have fun with....and be a friend with. I didn't think beyond friendship, and forgive me...I still don't. I would like to be your friend."

Lois let out a short sigh of relief. "Tom...that's so nice. I would love to have you for a friend."

They chatted for a couple of hours, learning many things about each other. Lois learned that Tom actually owned all that property he rented out, and that he was a very wealthy man. *Too bad there weren't sparks, eh, Lois?*

Shortly after Tom left, the boys ran into the house like they were being chased, and Lois wasn't sure she liked the look on their faces.

"What have you been doing? You all look guilty about something."

"No...we were just running so we would get here on time."

Although unconvinced, Lois let it drop. "There are some sodas in the fridge and some potato chips and corn curls in the cupboard." Her last word was drowned out as they stampeded toward the kitchen on a raid. She watched them—all three of them with too-long hair, in plaid flannel shirts and torn jeans—opening sodas and grabbing bags of snacks like they hadn't eaten in a week. *Teenagers.*

"Mom...who was here? Aunt Jackie?" Trent called

from the kitchen.

"No....you remember Tom from the beach? He stopped by since he was in Richmond for the day." Trent must have noticed the second cup in the sink.

"Cake! Mom! Did he bring this?" Yes, and if you want you all can have a piece."

It took all of five minutes for the boys to devour their pieces of cake, grab their sodas and snacks, and head toward Trent's bedroom. Lois had just finished watching the eleven o'clock news and was about to drop a movie into the DVD player, and the boys were playing the X-Box and listening to rap music on the stereo, when a sharp knock assaulted the front door. Lois opened the door to four deputies from the county sheriff's department, and her heart jumped into her throat.

"Ma'am, is Trent Watkins your son?"

"Yes," was all she could choke out. She knew this was trouble.

"Is he here?"

"Yes," she said again, and pointed toward the bedroom. "He and his two friends are in there." She was beginning to feel weak in the knees.

"Good....we got all three of them." The deputies moved toward the closed door and quickly opened it.

"Trent Watkins, Jason Blake, and Kevin McKnight....you're all under arrest."

Lois screamed and sank to the sofa. She couldn't breathe. What had they done? Oh God! Under arrest? Sobs tore from her throat as she covered her face. All three boys were put into handcuffs and were being led out the door. She couldn't watch. One of the deputies stayed behind to give her the details she would need.

"Ma'am? Are you all right?"

Lois stared at her trembling hands and gasped for air. "No...I'm not all right. What did they do?"

"They broke into a candy store...Holleran's Fine Candies up on Ridgeview. They didn't take anything because the alarm went off and they ran, but they did break the door. They won't be charged with robbery, just intent to rob, and breaking and entering." He handed her a glass of water he got out of the kitchen. "Here's where we are taking them. You may want to come down." The deputy handed Lois a card with the address on it, and she nodded.

"Do you want a ride?"

"No....I'll drive. Thanks," she responded.

The deputy left and closed the door behind him. *Oh God! Why? Why would he do this?* Lois's chest heaved up and down as she sobbed silently. Stumbling and staggering, like a dazed injured soul, she made her way to the kitchen and dialed Jackie's cell phone. Date or no date, Lois needed her *now*.

Chapter 23

Trent was facing Jason and Kevin at a table in a small room that had only one small window high up toward the ceiling. Two deputies, sitting on each end of the long table, stared at the boys as though they were waiting for them to make a run for it so they could pounce. Another deputy came through the door and pulled up a chair next to Jason. Trent caught a glimpse of his mother sitting on a bench, holding a wrinkled tissue in her hand, when the door opened. He could tell she had been crying, and he felt a sliver of remorse for what they had done.

"Trent, your mother is outside. Jason, we can't get in touch with your mother, and Kevin, your parents are on their way," the deputy informed them as he sat down. "When the other parents get here, we will have a meeting to discuss with them what is going to happen to the three of you." He was a big man, well over six feet, and much more than two-hundred-fifty pounds.

He took in the sight of all three boys at one time, without blinking, causing Trent to question whether he had eyelids. Trent almost laughed out loud when he silently compared him to a giant guppy.

The heavy steel door opened again, and another deputy stuck his head inside. "The McKnight's are here," he announced quietly.

The guppy nodded, and got up from his chair. Trent imagined that the chair gave a sigh of relief when he pushed it back and stood up. He was surprisingly light on his feet, Trent noticed, as he watched him walk out of the door.

"Well, Jason....all we're waiting on is your mother," the smaller and nicer of the deputies said.

"Did you look in the corner bar? The one near my house? That's probably where she is....getting sloshed. You might want to catch her before she brings home the latest loser and goes to bed with him."

Deputy Parker, according to his nametag, fixed his eyes on Jason for a moment, and there was the unmistakable look of pity in his eyes. "Okay....do any of you three want to tell me what you were thinking? That was a really stupid move." His eyes grazed over all three boys, one at a time, as he waited expectantly. "Jason? What do you have to say for yourself?"

Jason stared at the table, unmoving.

"Jason, you know this is your third offense, don't you?"

He nodded.

"Trent….second time around for you. What do you have to say about that? Nothing? What about your poor mother out there? She almost collapsed when we arrested you. Don't you think about what your antics do to her?"

Trent shrugged.

"Oh….and Kevin…..we have your priors. They were faxed to us from Michigan. How is it you have stayed out of jail this long?" He pulled out the bottom folder and opened it. "Assault, Assault again, robbery, breaking and entering, not to mention truancy. Man, kid….this is quite a lot of paper on you. You're how old? Fifteen?" Deputy Parker shook his head, sadly as the door opened again.

"They're all here now," the guppy deputy announced. The boys could hear Jason's mother shouting and swearing at the deputies, forcing an embarrassed Jason to put his head down on the desk. He knew she was probably three sheets to the wind. No wonder his dad left her. Who could stand that?

The door opened for a third time and the parents were being ushered in. Lois ran to Trent's side and sat down. "Are you okay?" she whispered. He nodded and she reached for his hand, more for comforting herself than him. He could feel her trembling.

Jason's mother came in swinging. She aimed an open-palmed slap against the side of Jason's head. "Dumb ass!" she shouted. The last to enter were the McKnight's. Kevin's mother was small and plain, her eyes darting back and forth like a frightened bird. His father looked stern as he narrowed his eyes at his son and tightened his jaw. "I've had enough," he growled at Kevin. Trent watched Kevin cower.

Just as the door was about to close, Jackie burst through it. A deputy stiff-armed her and made her stop in her tracks. "Who are you, Ma'am?" he asked.

"I'm her best friend," she answered, pointing at Lois.

"Well, you'll have to wait out there," he nodded toward the waiting area.

Jackie's eyes connected with Lois's. "I'll be right outside." Lois nodded.

The deputy in charge, Officer Guppy, as Trent thought of him, told the parents what the boys were being charged with.

"Why are you so sure it was these boys?" Rita Blake asked.

"Surveillance cameras, Ma'am. Their images were caught on camera and easily identified."

"But they didn't steal anything," Kevin McKnight Sr. confirmed.

"No….they ran…but breaking and entering is still an offense…not to mention damage to the store."

"So what happens now?" Lois asked, timidly.

"Well, they will be arraigned in the morning if we can get a judge, and more than likely charged. There is plenty of evidence to charge them." Lois began trembling and she tightened her grip on Trent's hand. "We're keeping them in custody tonight. You all can join them tomorrow at the arraignment. That's it. Parents, you can leave now," he instructed as he stood up and turned to two deputies standing just inside the door. "Take these boys to lock-up."

Lois began crying again.

"Mom, don't…okay? Don't cry." Trent spoke softly as he stood up and let the deputy place the handcuffs on him.

She watched him being led away and then stood on wobbly legs. Jackie was waiting for her on a bench outside the door, and a sobbing Lois dropped down beside her.

"Thanks for coming….oh God, Jackie…..what am I going to do?"

"He needs a lawyer, I think…" Jackie stopped talking when one of the deputies approached them.

"Mrs. Watkins, are you going to be all right? Hey….listen….we're making them stay in jail tonight as a lesson, hoping to scare them a little. We could have let them go home but we decided beforehand that these kids needed to see what jail was like."

If he thought this was going to make Lois feel better, he was sadly mistaken. She only cried harder, and he was at a loss as to what he should do or say. He sighed.

"Trent seems like an okay kid….and apparently you are a much better parent than the other kids have. Those other parents are already gone, yet you're still sitting here. Maybe a scare will put Trent back in line."

Lois nodded and wiped her nose. Jackie put her arm around Lois.

"Let's go. I'll stay at your house tonight, Lois….then we'll begin looking for a lawyer first thing in the morning. The arraignment isn't until eleven."

"Mrs. Watkins….may I suggest something?" Lois turned and stared at the deputy and waited for him to speak. "Don't agree to the court trying them all together. Make Trent have a separate trial." Again, Lois nodded.

Jackie followed Lois home and entered the kitchen just as Lois was putting water on for tea. Lois looked drained.

"Sorry for ruining your date tonight."

"That's okay. Terry was cool about it. In fact, he's on his way here now. He says you'll probably need to get Trent a lawyer and he knows one who is reasonable."

Lawyer! My baby needs a lawyer! "Yeah, I guess I will have to get a lawyer. God, Jackie...how did this happen? What am I not doing? What am I doing wrong?"

"I don't know, Lois....but maybe it's something you should ask Trent."

Chapter 24

When the two-month ordeal came to an end, Trent was sentenced to six hundred hours of community service, two years probation, and fines. Lois paid the fines and the attorney and that was the end of Trent's college fund. Terry's lawyer friend gave them a break on the fees, but it was still a substantial amount to pay out.

Lois and Trent left the courthouse together, after signing some paperwork. The ride home was relatively quiet until Trent asked, "I guess this means I can't get my license when I turn sixteen, doesn't it?"

"I believe that's true, Trent."

"I guess you heard that Jason was sent to juvie."

"Yeah, I did. His mother called me. She said she hoped you went with him. I'm just glad you didn't." Lois pulled into the driveway, shut the car off, and rested her head on the steering wheel.

Trent got out and slowly walked to the front door, glancing back once to see if Lois was going to follow. He went directly to his room and changed from his suit into a pair of cut-offs and a tee-shirt, and flopped down on his bed. He listened for the door to open again, letting his mother inside. He wished he could feel bad about how hurt and sad she was, and he wondered why he didn't. Admittedly, she was a great mom, but there was something missing. She loved him—loved him with her whole heart—but somehow that wasn't enough. He heard Lois come in and go straight to her room, probably to change. His mother had to take the day off from work today. He knew he should do something to try to make it all up to her, but he didn't know how. He got up and went to the kitchen and put on a pot of coffee. It was something he knew she would appreciate.

Lois came out of her room when she smelled the coffee, glancing at Trent as he stood at the stove.

"What are you doing?" She asked quietly.

"Making us some lunch. How does grilled cheese and tomato soup sound?" He turned to look at her, hoping he wouldn't see any tears. He was rewarded with a half-smile and soft eyes.

"That sounds fine. I'll set the table." Lois turned her back and completed the smile. Maybe she had her son back—*maybe*.

Once seated with their sandwiches and soup in

front of them, Lois casually asked, "Where do you want to do your community service? Have you thought about it?"

"No," he responded.

"Aunt Jackie says that her cousin works at the Humane Society, and if you're interested, she could get you in there. You like animals."

"Yeah….that might not be bad. That's on the list of places I can do, too, isn't it? Yeah…I'd like that. How do I get in there?"

"I'll call Aunt Jackie when she gets home from work and she'll find out for us."

Lois made the call and by the next day the arrangements were made. Trent was to report to the local Humane Society Shelter at nine o'clock the following Monday. Lois hoped Trent would enjoy the work and maybe develop some sense of responsibility while he was at it. Six hundred hours was a lot of hours. It was seventy-five eight-hour workdays, or twenty-five full days. It was going to take up a lot of Trent's time. Jason had been sent to a juvenile detention facility and Kevin's trial was tomorrow. Keeping the boys separated was probably a wise move at this point. From what she had heard about Kevin's history, he had quite a few violations. It looked like he would be going away, too.

Trent was lucky, and Lois only hoped he knew that.

She dropped Trent off at the animal shelter on her way to work on Monday. He seemed a little anxious about going, and Lois hoped it was just a case of nerves because it was a new experience for him. She watched him, with lunch bag in hand, walk toward the office, where he was told to report. The person she spoke to on the telephone on Friday told her there was a small lunchroom with a refrigerator and a microwave, so Trent could take meals to be heated if he wanted. Since it was summer, Trent could work forty hours if he wanted, but when school started in the fall, he would be limited to the weekends. He would find out his schedule today.

Trent walked into the small office and introduced himself to the woman standing at the counter. He thought she looked a little like Jackie, so he was not surprised when she told him she was Jackie's cousin, Bobbi Sue Johnson, and that he would report to her every day. She showed him around the offices first and then they went to the kennels. Trent's face lit up when he saw all the dogs and then the cats he would be around every day. He really *did* like animals and had often wished he had a pet.

"Okay....Trent...your job is going to be diversified

quite a bit here. You'll do what needs done, and some of it won't be all that pleasant. The feeding is done usually before nine and after five, so you really won't be feeding most of the residents here. However....you will be cleaning cages and kennels. Is that agreeable to you?"

"Yeah...I guess. I never did it before, but I think I can."

"Good...also...you'll be assisting in bathing and grooming some of the dogs, and upon occasion....assisting the vet when he comes in twice a week. Today we're just going to meet some of the residents and learn something about them. Oh...and you may be asked to help out at the counter when people buy things or pay the donations for the pets. We'll go over that later."

Trent decided he liked Bobbi Sue. She looked to be older than Jackie—forty, maybe—but she was still pretty and just as nice as Jackie. She told him she had been in charge of that facility for six years and just loved it. She took him around to each of the dog's kennels and told him something about each of them. There were so many homeless dogs! They broke for lunch and then visited the cats after that. There were just as many cats as there were dogs. He felt an immediate bond with a big grey cat with amber eyes, almost the color of his, and unceremoniously christened it with the name of

Riley. Yes, he was going to like it here.

When Lois came to pick him up at five o'clock Trent was surprised that the time had flown by so quickly. He talked about the shelter all the way home, amusing Lois with stories about some of the animals. She liked this new enthusiastic, talkative Trent—the one she thought she might never see again. Could she dare hope that things were going to turn around and Trent would be the great kid he had been before adolescence? Maybe—just maybe she could.

Chapter 25

Sunday was Trent's day off. He slept later than usual and got up when he smelled breakfast smells coming from the kitchen. He staggered out to the kitchen and was greeted by his mother's smile.

"Hi, sleepyhead….want some breakfast?" He nodded. "Five-hundred and fifty-two hours of community service to go, huh? How do you like it?"

"I do. I like it a lot," he mumbled sleepily. "Mom…can I bring home a cat?"

"A cat? I don't know, Trent. I never let you have a pet because I always worried about having to feed it and pay for vet bills."

"The one I want already has its shots and it's neutered already. I named him Riley…and…Mom, his eyes are the same color as mine. Can I bring him home?"

Lois set two plates on the table, one in front of Trent. "Yeah....I guess that would be okay. We'll have to get food and a litter box...some litter. Will you bring him home tomorrow?"

"If you'll let me....yeah."

"Well....then we better get some supplies for it today. Riley, you say? That's a nice name. What color is it?"

"Grey....he's all grey with golden eyes."

"Sounds pretty. I'll tell you what. We'll go to the store and pick up what we need and then go over to the Humane Society and get him today. How's that?"

"Cool! That'd be great!" Lois got the smile she had missed for the last few years.

After shopping for the new cat, they drove to the shelter. Bobbi Sue lit up when she saw Trent. "You're not working today, so you must be here to see Riley."

"Mom's letting me take Riley home."

"Wonderful! Let's go get him."

Trent and Lois followed Bobbi Sue down the aisles toward the cat section, and Lois just had to ask. "Trent, why a cat? I was afraid you would ask for a dog, and we aren't allowed to have a dog in the house."

"I know that. That's why I didn't pick out a dog. Besides, Riley's a great cat. He's almost as big as a dog."

Trent was right about that. The cat was a huge grey cat, probably a Russian Blue. Lois liked him immediately. They now had a pet. Trent introduced him to the litter box and the food dishes and then took the cat to his room, where Riley immediately curled up and took a nap. Lois sat at the kitchen table reading the Sunday paper while Trent napped alongside his new pet. It was a relaxing Sunday afternoon, until the telephone rang. Trent had just come out of his room, so he grabbed it first. Lois could only hear part of the conversation, and waited for the call to end.

"Who was that?"

"Kevin," Trent answered.

"Oh...where is he?"

"Home."

"Home? I thought his trial was almost two weeks ago."

"It was. He got probation."

"How did he manage that?"

"That's what it's like when your parents have money. Kevin's dad is a big attorney that works for the

State of Virginia. He got him off with just probation. He's coming over." Trent announced as he went back into his room.

Lois's heart sank. She had hoped to get Trent back on track without the influence of his friends, especially when one of them could practically get away with anything short of murder. Well, she was going to keep Trent at home. She was not going to allow him to take off with Kevin and do God only knew what.

It was a full ten minutes before she heard the knock on the door. She was surprised to find not only Kevin, but his father standing at the door.

"Mrs. Watkins, I hope it's okay for Kevin to visit. I brought him here but I wanted to talk to you before I just left him here." Lois waited for him to continue. "I don't want him leaving here until I pick him up, if that's okay."

"Yes, that's fine....preferable, actually."

"Good. Kevin, two hours....I'll be back in two hours."

Lois watched as the boy nodded in agreement, offered a weak smile to his father, and moved aside so Kevin could enter. Kevin went straight to Trent's room and Lois could hear the noisy greeting between them. She was annoyed to find Mr. McKnight still standing at the door. "Is there something you wanted to say, Mr.

McKnight?"

"Please call me Kevin, and yes....I just wanted you to know that Kevin will be attending a private boarding school in September, so he won't be around much. Just wanted you to know that."

"Thank you for telling me. That should be a good life experience for him."

"We're hoping," he responded with a tight-lipped sad smile and then left.

While the boys were in Trent's room Lois did some cleaning. She could hear the X-Box noise and so assumed that they were engaged in the game. *No harm there.* For some reason, she couldn't shake the sense of foreboding that came over her. What was it? Did she just not trust Kevin? That was probably it.

Trent and Kevin were engaged in the game on the X-Box, talking quietly while they played.

"Dude...my parents are going to try to make me go to a private boarding school."

"No friggin' way!" Trent responded.

"Yeah...they already signed the papers and paid my tuition. But guess what....I'm not going."

"How are you going to get out of it?"

"I'm taking off...that's how."

"When? And how?"

"I'm going to ask my dad if I can come over here on Wednesday. That's your day off this week, right?" Trent had been talking to Kevin since his trial, so Kevin knew when Trent worked.

"Yeah...right." Trent confirmed.

"Well...when he drops me off, I'm leaving." Trent and Kevin smiled at each other, silently making a pact.

Chapter 26

It was almost ten o'clock on Wednesday when Kevin's father came to pick him up. Trent answered the door when he knocked.

"Hi, Mr. McKnight...did Kevin forget something?"

"I'm sorry, Trent...I'm not sure what you mean." Kevin, Senior's stare was disapproving even if there was a hint of a plastic smile on his face. "I am here to pick him up. Is he ready to go?"

Trent wrinkled his brow as if in concentration and his eyes drifted to the carpet. "Now I'm not sure what *you* mean," he said, looking puzzled. "You picked him up a half hour ago...didn't you?"

Kevin McKnight pushed his way past Trent and strode across the living room. He pushed Trent's bedroom door open and quickly surveyed the room. "Where is he?" He turned his stormy eyes on Trent.

"Don't play with me, kid...where is he?"

"I....I don't know. He said you were outside and he grabbed his stuff and left. I went into the bathroom just as he was going out the door."

"Bullshit! You expect me to believe that?" he shouted at Trent.

Lois heard the shouting and ran into the living room from the laundry room. "What's going on? Kevin....Trent....what happened?"

"Did you see my son leave here?"

"Yes, I did. He said goodnight to me and said his dad was outside. He left about...a half hour ago....wasn't it, Trent?"

"Yeah, Mom....that's what I told Mr. McKnight, but he doesn't believe me."

"You weren't outside waiting for him?"

"NO! I just got here. Trent, did he say anything to you about going somewhere?"

"No....not really."

"Not really....what exactly does that mean?"

"Well...he didn't want to go to a boarding school....and he said..."

"What? What did he say?"

"He said he'd rather go live on the streets than go to some stuffy boarding school. He said that on Sunday. He said if you and his mom didn't want him any more, he could just leave and save you the cost of tuition. But he didn't actually say he was going to go."

Kevin's father mumbled a few expletives and opened his cell phone. First, he called his wife and then he called the police. Kevin's mother, Janet McKnight was on her way over. She arrived just before the officer came to take a report. Lois put on a pot of coffee. Even if nobody else needed a cup, she was going to. While the coffee was brewing, she set out some cookies and pastries and offered up her kitchen table for everyone to sit around. Trent, she noticed, chose to stay close to her, which was just fine by her. Kevin's father was a very intimidating man, and judging from the wide-eyed frightened stare on Janet McKnight's face, Lois and Trent weren't the only ones who thought so.

The police officer opened his notebook, readied his pen, and then looked around the room. "So....who saw him last?" All eyes went to Trent.

"I did..." Trent responded, clearly uncomfortable with the situation.

"So tell me about what he said; what he did."

"We were playing a game...on the X-Box....that was all. Then he said his dad was outside...he grabbed his stuff and left."

"What stuff did he have?" The officer prodded.

"Just a kind of duffel bag with things in it."

"What things?" The officer continued to probe.

"I don't know what was in it. It was full of something. Mr. McKnight brought him over. I would think he would know what was in the bag." Trent silently congratulated himself on the deflection when all eyes went to Kevin's dad.

Kevin McKnight, Senior cleared his throat. "He told me he was returning some things you had lent him, since he would be going away to boarding school."

"I never lent Kevin anything."

"Son, do you have any idea where he may have gone?" The police officer softened toward Trent.

"No, sir...I don't have any idea, but I know he talked a lot about missing his friends in Michigan."

"Well, that's a place to start, anyway. Mr. and Mrs. McKnight, I'll need a good description, a picture, and any other information you can provide. I'll be at your house in about a half hour."

Trent was relieved that he was out of the line of fire for awhile. He knew there would probably be more questioning, but for now, he was feeling very smug. He knew where Kevin had gone, and he knew how he was going to get there. Michigan was the furthest place from Kevin's destination, but planting that seed had been the plan—and it worked. As Kevin's parents and the police officer filed out, Riley came into the kitchen and jumped on Trent's lap. Lois joined Trent and Riley after she shut the door.

"Trent, do you know where Kevin went?"

Trent, looked her in the eye, and said, "No, Mom....I don't." It was the first blatant lie he ever told her. He stroked Riley as he kept from making eye contact again. He used the only way he knew to get away from the subject. "Mom, you know....Riley and I have a lot in common. He doesn't know his father either." Lois felt the little jab pierce her heart, but she let it pass. "We have the same eyes. Mom, maybe we have the same father."

"Don't be absurd, Trent. That's just plain silly."

"I just meant that our eyes are so much alike and yet my eyes are a very uncommon color for humans. Aren't they?"

"Yes, I suppose they are."

"Are they exactly like my father's eyes?"

"Yes, they are. Your hair is darker, but other than that, you look almost exactly like him. You're thinner, too."

"Did he have any particular talents or anything? Something I might have inherited?"

Oh, yes...he had a talent, but I'm certainly not going to share that with you, my darling son. "Well, he played football in high school, and he could draw."

"Well, forget the football, but I can draw. Do you think I got that from him?"

"Well, since I can't, I guess you did get it from him. He was also very smart."

"Ha! I guess I didn't inherit that then, did I?" *Although I am smart enough to get away from the subject of Kevin.*

Chapter 27

With Kevin gone and Jason still in the detention center, Trent had a lot of free time after his hours at the animal shelter. He began drawing pictures, and many of them were quite good. He sketched Riley in various positions, and then did some sketches of the other animals at the shelter from memory. Lois was impressed with his art, and suggested that he consider going to school to study art after he graduated. Even though she was glad that he was staying home, she was also concerned about his sullenness. He seemed to be brooding all the time, and lethargic most of the time. He ate his meals in silence, only responding to questions in as few words as possible. Was he becoming depressed? Lois wondered.

Trent's eleventh grade year began at the end of August. He went to school and immediately went to the animal shelter afterward. Lois picked him up after she left work at four-forty-five. He had completed a little more than half of his community service hours, and hoped to complete the rest of the hours by his birthday. If he made it to the shelter every day, he would be able to fulfill his goal.

He had heard from Kevin twice. He had called the week before school started. It was a Wednesday, Trent's day off. Kevin told him he was in Florida and working at a restaurant on the beach. He found a room at a place where nobody checked up on anybody, but he was keeping a low profile anyway. "Dude...why don't you come down?" He had asked. Trent declined, with the excuse that he was planning on going to look for his father. "Hey, Dude....my dad's a dick. Are you sure you want to know yours?" Trent told him that he was sure, and Kevin wished him luck. He called once more to ask Trent if he heard anything about whether they were still looking for him.

Trent knew they were still looking. The police had been to the house to question Trent more than once. Trent kept to his story that he had no idea where Kevin was.

But Kevin was not Lois's concern. Trent was. She tried several times to draw him out of the dismal state that seemed to envelop him. Christmas was approaching and Lois hoped that he would snap out of his funk.

"Trent, what would you like for Christmas this year?" she began.

"Nothing, except to meet my father." His answer was quick and to the point.

"Other than that," Lois sighed.

"Then nothing," he answered sharply.

"Trent, we have been over this before. I don't know where your father is."

"Have you tried looking for him?"

"Yes....yes, Honey, I have. Everything is a dead end. I even searched the Internet with a people finders program. All I know is his name and that he was from the Pittsburgh area. I realize how much you want to know who he is, and if I could find him, I would. It's been sixteen years, Trent. I'm afraid the trail is cold. Why is it so important to you? I've tried to be the best parent I could be."

"Mom...yes, you are. But a kid wants to know where he came from. There are things I want to know....about me...about him. Do I have cousins...brothers...sisters? Who are my grandparents? You don't even have any relatives of your own....except your brother....who hates us because I was born out of wedlock. He's a jerk, anyway...so I don't care if we don't see him. My grandparents were gone before I was even thought about...so I don't have any relatives...except my father...and his relatives. They probably don't even know anything about me, but I want to know something about them."

Lois's heart just broke. Trent hadn't spoken this many words at one time in a very long time—and his words were full of pain and anxiety. If only she could afford a private investigator. "Is this why you're so sullen all the time, Trent? It means that much to you?"

"Well, yeah, Mom...you knew your mother *and* your father; didn't you? Don't you think I would want to know both of my parents?"

"I'll see what I can do, Trent. I'll ask someone about digging deeper into a search for him. I don't know what else to tell you, but I can't promise anything." She hoped this would appease him, but she doubted it. Until today, she had no idea how tormented Trent was about not knowing his father.

Christmas came and Christmas went, and Trent remained sullen. He returned to school after the holiday break and then he turned sixteen two weeks later. Lois tried to make his birthday special. She offered to let him have a party but he declined the idea. He settled for dinner in a nice restaurant, just the two of them.

Lois missed the old Trent—the one with the easy smile and sparkle in his eyes. The only time he had any spark in his eyes was when he held Riley. He seemed to have no interest in anything, and his grade report showed it. He barely passed anything. When Lois stared at the grade report showing all D's and one C, she didn't know what to say.

"Why, Trent? There is no excuse for grades like these. You're not stupid. I want you to start hitting the books more. You'll never get into a college with grades like these."

"Maybe I don't want to go to college."

"Honey, why not? College is essential nowadays."

"We can't afford it anyway....remember? You had to use my college fund to pay my fines and my attorney."

"But since then I have put more money into the fund, so it's growing again. Of course you'll need loans, but college is not out of the question."

Trent didn't answer her, but just went into his room and shut the door. The next day he was gone.

Carole McKee

Chapter 28

The tears just kept coming, non-stop. Lois sat at the kitchen table, with Jackie at her side and a box of tissues in front of her. A lead weight pressed down on her chest as she watched the officer read the note Trent left:

Mom, I'm sorry. You're a great mom, but I have to find him.

Love, Trent

"When did you discover he was gone?" the officer asked.

"This morning, about an hour ago. I called for him to get up for school and there was no response. I heard his cat crying so I opened the door....and the room....was e-empty..." Lois began sobbing. Then....then I saw the note...and...and...." She couldn't finish.

"Who does he have to find? Kevin McKnight?"

"NO...his father. He is obsessed with knowing him."

"Does he know where to look?"

"Only...only that his father was from Pittsburgh. He...he may try to get there."

The officer shook his head and began writing on his yellow legal pad. "Kids. They always want what they can't have, especially when it comes to their parents. I was the same way when I was young. My mother wasn't married when she had me and all I ever wanted was for my father to show up. Of course, he never did. I ran away to look for him myself once. Got hauled back home by the seat of my pants by a local sheriff. He scared the daylights out of me and I never ran away again. I know that's not much consolation to you."

"Thank you....it helped, believe it or not. I guess I feel as though I failed him in some way. I...I..." Lois couldn't say anything more, as she began to crumble. Jackie grabbed her hand and gently squeezed it, letting go when someone knocked at the door. Jackie let another officer pass through the door and offered him coffee as he sat down. Before he could accept or decline she set a cup in front of him. He smiled at Jackie and turned to Lois.

"We're going to put an APB out on him. I'll need a picture to scan for the cars. We just got the computers in our cars, but the State and the County have had them for quite awhile. It's very convenient. They can pull the picture up any time they see a kid that resembles his description. Do you know what he was wearing?"

"He would have his black and red parka on. It's mostly black with red trim. It's a regular quilted parka with a hood; probably he would be wearing jeans, and carrying a black and white sports bag. That's what is missing from his closet." Lois handed him a recent picture of Trent and the officer thanked her and stood up.

"Let me get this on a scanner ASAP," he said, and then downed the rest of the coffee in his cup. Jackie saw him out the door.

"Don't worry, Mrs. Watkins….we'll find him. If he's on foot he hasn't gotten too far. Problem is that we're supposed to get another snow storm and the temperature is supposed to drop. The elements are going to be against him." The officer handed her a card as he stood up. "Call us if you hear anything."

Lois nodded and reached for the card. "Thank you. Please….find him. He's all I have and I love him so much."

"I know you do, Ma'am. It's a pleasure to meet loving parents who actually care about their kids. Problem is....even if you love them, you can't always know what they're going to do." He smiled at her and let himself out.

Jackie set a plate of toast in front of Lois. "Eat something. I know your stomach is in knots, but try."

Lois looked at the toast as if it were a plate of worms. She was not going to be able to swallow anything. She jumped when the telephone rang. Jackie answered it on the second ring. "No, we don't want to order the newspaper," Jackie hung up. "Telephone sales call," she told Lois.

Lois sat by the telephone all morning and into the afternoon, just hoping to hear something. The police called once to say they had no leads yet, and Terry, Jackie's boyfriend came by around lunch time. Jackie was making soup to go with the ready-made sandwiches Terry brought from the deli.

"Where could he be, Jackie?" Lois was crying again.

"I wish I knew, Honey. I'd go get him myself, if I did. And then I'd give him an ear-beating he would never forget....after I hugged him."

Trent was cold. He had been walking in a northerly

direction for hours, minus the time he stopped to warm up and have a cup of hot chocolate at a donut shop. He should have gotten a donut while he was there, because now he was starving. There hadn't been any sign that he might run into a fast food restaurant any time soon, either. He knew he should go back, but he couldn't. He needed to find his father.

His mother knew by now that he was gone, and she was probably in hysterics. That made him feel bad, but his mother didn't seem to understand how badly he needed to know his father.

He couldn't feel his feet any more. Maybe this was a bad idea. He was hungry, cold, and tired—so tired from walking, and to make matters worse—it was snowing. He needed to sit down somewhere. Not far up the road, lights were reflecting off of the dark snow clouds. It had to be some type of establishment— maybe food. He continued to walk toward the lights in the sky. Yes! It was the light from the golden arches bouncing off the clouds! McDonald's was within his reach! His legs picked up speed as he headed toward that direction. So intent on getting inside, he didn't see the police cars until it was too late.

Just as he got to the parking lot, two state troopers cut him off. One trooper was out of the car and had him in custody before Trent's frozen brain registered what was happening. He was put into the back of the car, and almost welcomed the heat blasting inside the car.

"Hey! I'm starving! Can I get something to eat before you arrest me?"

"Arrest you? We're not arresting you. We're taking you home to your mama. Do you know what you have done to her, you little idiot?"

The trooper didn't say another word, which suited Trent just fine. Before too long he dozed off in the back of the police car and didn't awaken until the car pulled into his driveway.

Chapter 29

It was dark outside, when the telephone rang. Lois grabbed it up, her heart pounding in her chest.

"Mrs. Watkins? We have him. A trooper is bringing him home. They should be there shortly," the male voice assured her.

"Thank you...oh, thank you," Lois whispered breathlessly as she hung up the phone. Tears of gratitude spilled over onto her cheeks.

"Lois, there's a police car pulling into the driveway," Jackie called to her and then ran to the door. "It's him! They have him!"

Jackie and Lois watched as the state trooper opened the back door and ushered Trent out of the car. Holding onto his arm, the trooper walked with him up to the door. Sobbing hysterically, Lois flung the door open and reached for Trent. "Oh Trent....please don't do this again....please!" she wailed.

"Mom...stop crying...please," he responded. The sound of his voice brought Riley out of the bedroom, meowing. Trent picked him up and walked toward the kitchen, still wearing his coat and boots. He set Riley down and took off his coat, and then sat to remove his boots. Jackie followed him to the kitchen. "Are you hungry?" she asked.

"Starving. Is that broccoli cheese soup I smell?"

"It is. Sit down and I'll get you a bowl. How about a sandwich to go with it? I'm going to beat your ass right after you eat, so enjoy."

"Aunt Jackie, I didn't mean to hurt my mother...but I have to know my father. I have to! She doesn't understand that. Maybe he was just a fling to her, but to me, it's my heritage. I want to know more about him than just his eye color."

"Trent....what if he is a jerk? What if he's someone who doesn't like kids?"

"Do you really think my mother would have fallen for him if that's true? And it's not the point. The point is...I can't say that about him. Kevin said his dad is a dick...because he knows his dad. I can't say anything...because I don't know if he is a good guy or a bad guy. It's like living in some kind of shell...or like when someone asks you what your dad does for a living. I can't answer that because I just don't know. And it hurts, Aunt Jackie. It just hurts."

Lois spoke to the state trooper for a few minutes, and thanked him again as he opened the door to leave. The trooper stared at her for a moment, his hand on the door.

"Mrs. Watkins, he's not a bad kid...just a little lost and confused."

Lois nodded and thanked him before she shut the door. She had heard every word Trent had spoken to Jackie and it broke her heart. The consequences of that night of passion went deeper than an unplanned pregnancy and becoming a single parent. Her son, who she loved more than life itself, was suffering the consequences of that night. Well, she had to do something. Maybe it would be futile but she had to try. She straightened her spine and quietly walked into the kitchen. Trent looked up when she sat down across from him, and Lois saw the sadness in his eyes.

"Are you okay?"

"Just cold and hungry. I'm sorry, Mom."

"I know you are. I'm sorry, too. It's my fault that you're going through this torment....and I'm going to do something about it."

Jackie put a bowl of soup and a spoon in front of Lois, and she stopped talking long enough to taste it. "Very good, Jackie." She told her.

"What is it you're going to do, Mom?"

"When school is out for the summer...we're taking a trip to Pittsburgh...to look for your father....but on one condition..."

"Really? What's the condition?" He asked warily, quelling his excitement for the moment.

"I want the grades brought up to at least all C's. If you can do that, we will drive to Pittsburgh and see if we can find him."

"Is that a promise, Mom?"

"Only if the grades come up."

"Okay....I think I can do that." Trent smiled at her and then grinned, warming her heart. It was the first time in a long time she had witnessed that grin.

They would make that trip. She owed Trent that much. Hopefully the outcome wouldn't be more painful than what Trent was experiencing right now. Lois mentally began planning the trip and—okay—what she would say to Jonathan if they found him.

Chapter 30

Nelson Sutter was being led to the private visitors' room where attorneys and clients were allowed to meet. He was utterly shocked when he was told he had a visitor, since he had never had one before. When he saw where they were headed he realized his attorney must be waiting for him, but he couldn't imagine why. Dave had been his attorney before his troubles and then twice for his sentencing, but since he had been incarcerated, he had made no contact.

The guard stopped and unlocked the door, standing aside so Nelson could enter. Now he was doubly surprised--not just his attorney sat at the table but right beside him sat Loraine! He paused and gave a quick grin before he walked into the room and sat down across from them.

"Dave...and Loraine....this *is* a surprise. What brings you here?"

Dave cleared his throat and glanced at Loraine. "We have some news for you. Loraine, why don't you tell him?"

"All right...I...guess I should be the one to tell him. Nelson, you have a son."

"What? What do you mean? Who? I mean...I don't know what I mean, I guess. Can one of you explain it to me? Who is the mother?"

Loraine let out a sigh. How sad it is that he doesn't have a clue who he fathered a child with, Loraine thought silently. "When you went looking for Lindy, do you remember spending the night in Richmond? Does the name Lois mean anything to you?"

"Lois? Lois! Yes, I remember her. She actually wrote to me, but you know that. You got the letters."

"Yes...addressed to Jonathan Riley. I knew they were for you. It was sick of you to use Lindy's last name."

"The name just came to me...I don't know why I did it."

"And told the girl I was your mother. Nice, Nelson."

"Yeah, that was pretty rotten. Sorry. So what about Lois?"

"She's in Pittsburgh...with her son...your son."

"How can you be sure he's mine?"

"He looks like you...and he has the eyes....gold, like yours."

"Yeah? So why now....after all this time...would she come looking for me? That kid would be what? About sixteen now."

"She said she didn't tell you about the baby when she wrote because she didn't want you to think she was asking for anything. She kept hoping that you would write her back or get in touch with her....but you didn't...so she just raised him herself."

"That still doesn't explain why now."

"Well, the boy is troubled...tormented...over not knowing his father. He...just wants to know who his father is. He ran away last winter. He was going to try to find you, but the police found him first and took him home. His mother has been through it with him. He's broken her heart a couple of times."

"Lois. I remember....we went to a carnival together. She was fun and funny...sweet...a really good person."

"Yeah, you seem to prey on those kinds."

"Used to, anyway," Nelson said softly, smiling a little. "You're right, Loraine...I was no prince."

"No, you sure weren't. Anyway…the boy wants to meet his father."

"I can't…..Loraine…I can't meet him in here. That's just not possible…not fair. It's not fair to him or to me. Damn it! I really would have liked to have had a son. Things may have been different…I don't know."

"Nelson…you can't just not see him. It would be like you're not acknowledging him….like you don't want him. The kid is suffering."

"Yeah, I seem to bring that on with a lot of people, don't I?"

Loraine let out an exaggerated sigh. "Yes, you do. And besides, the kid knows you're in jail. Lois wants to see you first before you meet Trent."

"Trent? That's his name?"

"Trent Riley Watkins, to be exact. He's a good looking boy. Artistic, sensitive…he has a very gentle nature about him, but he's sullen and withdrawn."

Nelson's attorney opened his briefcase and pulled out a calendar. "Nelson, I'll set it up for tomorrow. I'll bring Lois with me and we'll meet in a room like this. If all goes well, we can set it up for the day after. How would that be?"

Nelson Sutter couldn't sleep. Tomorrow he would meet the mother of his child, and then the next day, he would meet his child—his son. He looked forward to it and dreaded it at the same time. Although he wanted to meet him, he knew he would be a disappointment to him. Nelson reflected on the memories of his own dad. His dad was always there for him—loved him, even though his mother didn't. He would like to be able to say he had been there for his son all those years. He wished he had written to Lois. Maybe they should have gotten together. He might not be in prison right now had he bothered to answer her letters.

He rolled over for the umpteenth time and tried to get comfortable. Finally, he dozed and dreamt of a boy—a smiling boy who called him 'Dad.'

The meeting was set up for ten in the morning. Nelson took an early shower, brushed his teeth, and combed his hair, trying to look as presentable as he could. As he recalled, Lois was a very pretty girl with a sweet southern drawl. As he sat waiting for the guard to come for him, he wondered if she was still attractive. He had no idea how old she was, he realized. He remembered her green eyes and auburn hair, and her sexy figure. He anticipated seeing her, but at the same time, he was uncomfortable about it. He was now fifty-five, going on fifty-six, and looking it. Trent might not be the only one disappointed in him, he realized as he watched the guard walk closer to his cell.

"You have a visitor again, Sutter. You've suddenly gotten very popular. You running for office or something?" The guard joked. Nelson laughed lightly and let the guard lead him to the visitors' room a second time.

The guard unlocked the door and there she was—sitting there looking just as hot as ever. *Sweet Jesus, why did I let her get away?*

"Lois..."

"Jonathan....or....I mean, Nelson. I...don't know what to call you....or what to say. How are you?" Lois stumbled over her words.

"I'm incarcerated. I don't have to ask how you are. You are fine...gorgeous. So I have a son? Why didn't you tell me?"

"If you would have written to me I would have told you. I didn't want to pressure you into something you didn't want. I mean...if you didn't write back, you didn't want me...and if you didn't want me, you probably didn't want a child either."

"But now you're here. And he wants to meet me?"

"Yes...it's been an obsession of his to find you."

"You know…I've thought about you a lot over the years, Lois. I figured you were married with about three kids by now."

"I never married, Nelson. Trent was kind of a full time responsibility."

"I'm sure he was, Honey. I'm so sorry I wasn't a part of his life. I'll regret that for the rest of my life. I owe you something, Lois. I don't know how I'm going to do it, but I owe you. He is half mine and I plan on making it right….somehow."

Lois's eyes became brilliant with unshed tears. "Just see what you can do for Trent. He needs to know he has a father that cares about him. He knows you didn't know about him. I was honest with him about that. He doesn't know that it was just a one-night stand."

"And he won't know that…ever. Lois…it was only one night because I had to go. If I could have, I would have gone back for you. I planned on it, but then I got arrested."

Lois nodded. "That's nice to hear…even if it's not true."

"But it is true. Lois, you'll come back to see me, won't you?"

"I'll be bringing Trent with me tomorrow, Nelson," Dave interjected.

"But Lois, you'll come back...please?"

"Okay...yes...I'll come back, Nelson. I don't know how long I'll be in Pennsylvania but I'll come back and visit while I'm here."

"Thank you," Nelson responded with a smile and then reached for her hand. He held onto it for a moment, wanting more. He wanted to hug her but that was not permitted. Until this moment, Nelson did not realize how much he missed human contact, especially feminine human contact.

Chapter 31

The meeting with Trent was set up for one o'clock the very next day. It was another sleepless night for Nelson. The anticipation was killing him. He wanted to meet this boy—have a father-son relationship with him, but how was that going to happen from prison? Maybe it was too late to teach him how to ride a bike, play baseball, or help him with his elementary school homework, but he could be a father figure in his life, if he weren't in prison. Regret flooded over him like water coming through a broken levy. All this time wasted because he couldn't let go of his obsession with Lindy and her family. Obsession—well, he guessed his son and he had that in common. Lois said Trent was obsessed with finding his father.

"Maybe I'm jumping the gun here," he mumbled quietly. "The kid will probably be disappointed and not want anything to do with me after he meets me." *Who could blame him? His father is a major screw-up who*

harmed a young girl and then took her young child.
Nelson shifted his weight on top of his cot and stared at
the cold, grey wall.

Silently, he spoke. "Now I know how I hurt you
when I took Samantha, Lindy. Now I know what it feels
like to have a child you can't touch. If you think jail is
punishment enough, you are wrong, Lindy. This
punishment is way above and beyond cruel and unusual
punishment. Now I may never have the chance to be a
dad to my kid."

Nelson got up from his cot, quickly walked over to
his small writing desk that was attached to the opposite
wall, and wrote those thoughts and feelings down on
his yellow legal-sized tablet. Somehow, by writing it
down, he could put it in perspective.

It was time. Nelson's breath caught in his throat as
he heard the guard coming toward his cell. "Sutter,
you're going to the visitation room again. Are you sure
you're not running for office?"

Nelson laughed. "I just found out I have a son I
never knew about. I'm about to meet him...become a
dad," he confided.

"That's some heavy stuff, Sutter. How did you
manage not to know about it?"

"The woman was in another state. She wrote to me but I didn't get the letters until much later…and even then there was nothing in the letters about a kid." The guard favored him with a lopsided smile and they began the journey toward the visitors' room.

Outside the door, Nelson waited as the guard unlocked the door. Through the dirty wired glass he could see two people sitting at the table, waiting for him. He recognized one as Dave, his attorney, so the other must be his son—his boy. Nelson felt his heart begin to race and his mouth went dry. Of all the meetings, confrontations, and appointments he had been involved with in his life, this was the biggest, most important one he had ever anticipated. His son was behind this door! Nelson tightened his spine as the door opened. He was there, sitting at the table with his forearms resting on it. Nelson walked forward, just swallowing the boy with his eyes. He couldn't help the smile that spread across his face when he immediately recognized that his son looked just like him.

"Trent. I don't know what to say. You are obviously my son and it's nice to meet you. I guess I should say I'm sorry for not meeting you sooner."

"Mom said you didn't know about me." Trent challenged.

"She's right….I didn't. If I had known about you, I

would have been in contact with you way before this. I'm sorry I haven't been there for you. I wish I could have been. I know I must be a disappointment to you and I'm sorry for that. I made a few big mistakes. I just wasn't thinking rationally for a long time."

"Are you sorry for what you did?"

"Oh yeah...especially now, knowing that I have a son I should have been there for. It's been rough, huh?"

"No....not really...I mean....mom's great...but I just wanted to know who the other half of me was....you know?"

"Yeah, I do know. What would you like to know about me? I mean you already know I'm a major screw-up."

"I can draw really well. Did I get that from you?"

Nelson smiled. "Yeah, I guess you did. What do you like to draw?"

"Animals, mostly."

"That's what I always liked to draw." Nelson swallowed hard. A lump the size of a golf ball had formed in his throat and he had to look away.

The attorney, who had been sitting there quietly through the exchange, cleared his throat. "Nelson, this kid looks exactly like you, except his hair is a little darker. Same chin and jaw line, eyes, nose...even your hands are the same."

Nelson quickly averted his eyes down to Trent's hands and then looked at his own. Their hands were almost identical in shape and size, including the short wide fingers. Working man's hands, his father had called them.

"So where did you grow up?" Trent asked.

"On a farm in Central Pennsylvania. My father was the foreman and my mother was the local emergency nurse and midwife."

"Did you like it?"

"Yeah, it was okay. I liked taking care of the animals. We had cows, two goats, chickens, two horses, and some pigs. The pigs stunk really bad."

Trent laughed. "I have a cat. I got him because he has eyes the same color as mine. I named him Riley, because I thought that was your name."

Nelson chuckled. "Yeah, I was a real jerk. Your mother is one of the sweetest, nicest people I have ever met. I should have told her my real name, but I was going by an alias at the time. Your mother deserved better than that...and so did you. Tell me about where you're growing up."

"It's okay. We rent a small house in a pretty decent neighborhood. Mom works hard to keep it but we don't really have a lot of money. Our car is about to die, as usual."

"Do you like school?"

"Sometimes. I like my art classes, but it's hard going to school when you don't have money for things. I mean, mom gives me everything she can, but...I still need things I haven't told her about. We have to buy a lot of our own art supplies."

Nelson stared down at the table and bit his lip. He could have been helping with all of that. *Chock up one more failure and one more ruined life.*

"Do you have friends?"

"A couple. My best friend is in juvie and my other best friend ran away. He hasn't been found yet."

"Any girls?"

"Here and there. Mom has a cow over girls." Trent told him about the two girls at the beach, and Nelson tried not to laugh. That brought back a few memories. "I didn't have any friends in elementary school. One kid said I was a bastard and nobody should play with me...so nobody did."

That broke Nelson's heart and made him angry at the same time. *How dare someone call his son a bastard?* "I'm sorry. That wasn't very fair, was it?" He consoled.

Trent shrugged. "After awhile I was used to it. Mom went after some kid's dad once for calling me that. She always stuck up for me when I needed her."

"That's good....I'm glad." Nelson was close to crying right then, but he heard the jingle of keys outside the door, and then the door swung open.

"Five more minutes, Sutter," the guard reminded him.

"Okay," Nelson responded and then turned to Trent. "Will you come back? We have lots to learn about each other. I want to know everything about you. Will you give me a chance to do that?" Trent nodded and stood up. Nelson realized that his son was about the same height as he was at that age. Without thinking, he rushed around the table and wrapped his arms around Trent, hugging him tightly. "Somehow I am going to find a way to make everything up to you," he whispered. Trent hesitated, and then hugged him back.

Nelson went back to his cell and lay down on his cot. His emotions were getting the best of him, so he just buried his face in the pillow and let loose with the tears. Finally, after most of his life had passed, he found the one thing he should have been living for.

Trent walked out of the jail and got into Dave's car. He was quiet on the ride home and only spoke to thank Dave for taking him. Just before he pulled out of Loraine's driveway, Dave agreed to pick him up in two days and take him back to see Nelson. Loraine had been kind enough to let them stay with her while they were in the Pittsburgh area. Lois and Loraine were at the kitchen table when he went inside.

"How'd it go, Honey?" Lois asked.

At first, Trent didn't answer. He leaned against the kitchen door frame and stared at the floor, and then he suddenly looked up at Lois, grinning. There was that spark in his eyes that had been gone for the past few years. "I met my dad. That's how it went."

Chapter 32

Trent couldn't sleep. He had finally met the man who had sired him—his father—his dad. He had a dad! Did that mean he wasn't a bastard any more? He doubted that was true, since his father didn't marry his mother. He briefly wondered about that. They both said really great things about each other, so why had they not gotten married? He was going to have to ask his father, since his mother had never volunteered that kind of information.

Trent rolled onto his back and placed his arms under his head. His father seemed like a nice guy. It was hard to believe that he had admittedly done all those things that got him convicted. Was there any chance of parole and when would that be? Would his father consider marrying his mother? Nelson looked to be a lot older than his mother. Was that because of the hard life he led or was he just that much older? There were many things he wanted to know.

Nelson apologized for being such a disappointment. Trent thought about that. Was he disappointed? Yes and no. Of course he was disappointed that his father was in prison. He had hoped for a successful man with all the charisma of a movie star and a heart of gold who would just shower him with all the things rich kids had. But Nelson obviously accepted him and regretted not being there for him. He didn't have the success and the money, but he certainly had the heart. That was one out of three—right?

He rolled over and finally dozed off, waking when the sun came blindingly through the bedroom blinds. He could hear movement in the kitchen and assumed that both Lois and Loraine were awake and probably drinking coffee. He quickly dressed and went to the kitchen to find only Loraine sitting at the table reading the morning paper.

"Well, good morning, Trent. Sleep well?"

"No, not really...I had things on my mind."

Loraine's eyes softened. "I'm sure you did. Would you like some breakfast?"

"Just cereal would be fine. Would you like me to cut your grass for you today? I see it's getting high. I mean....you're letting us stay here and all. I could help out."

"That's very kind of you, but I have a lawn service coming today. They come every week. Trent...I can't imagine what you think about all of this with your dad, but maybe I can help you with some things."

"Like what things?"

"Well, I was married to him. Nelson could be the greatest guy in the world at times...actually, most of the time. But he just had, for some ungodly reason, an obsession with Lindy. If he had never met her, he may still be free today. But then he would still be married to me and probably would have never met your mother. Everything happens for a reason, I guess. Who can really understand the plan?" Loraine watched him prepare a bowl of cereal and carry it to the table. He went back for a spoon and then sat down.

"What was the deal with Lindy? Who was she?"

"She was our foster daughter. She was lovely. Something about her triggered something in Nelson. I found out years later that she was the daughter of his teenage fantasy. He had been in love with Lindy's mother all through high school and even after that. He was not aware that Lindy was her daughter though. Lindy looked exactly like her mother and somehow that triggered Nelson's reaction to her."

"That sounds crazy," Trent countered.

"Yes, it does. Nelson did not have a very good childhood. His mother hated him and was cruel beyond words. He had low self-esteem which actually produced some wonderful, lovable qualities in him, but it also created the obsession with first, Lindy's mother and then Lindy. Nelson loved Stacey silently for years, but he thought he wasn't good enough for her. By the time Lindy came to live with us, Nelson was successful and figured he was finally good enough for Stacey, but settled for Lindy…Stacey's look-alike. I hate what he did to Lindy, because I loved her so much. Anyway…I probably shouldn't have told you all that. Maybe Nelson didn't want you to know all the details."

"I'm glad you did. I know what it's like feeling you're not good enough. I feel that way all the time. Where is my mom anyway?"

"She is meeting with the attorney this morning. I don't know how long it will be."

"I would like to meet Lindy. Do you think I could?" Trent's eyes—Nelson's eyes—imploringly penetrated Loraine's.

"Well, I don't know, Honey. Lindy was pretty traumatized by Nelson….and Ricky, her husband was angry enough to kill him. I suppose I could talk to them to see how they would feel about meeting Nelson's son. I think it would certainly make Nelson more human to them."

"Would you talk to them? I mean, Dave said that if Lindy would agree to it, my dad could possibly get a lighter sentence….maybe paroled or even get moved to a place that wasn't so tightly secured."

"I'll see what I can do for you." Loraine smiled.

"Do you hate my dad?"

"Heavens, no. I did for a little while…well, maybe for a lot longer than that…but I don't any more. Your father made a couple of major mistakes…but he has a lot of good qualities. I have a lot of happy memories from the time we spent together."

"What was he like? I mean when you were married to him?"

"Well, let's see. He was always considerate….pleasant….and he helped out around the house a lot. I remember going shopping with him. He seemed to enjoy it, and he always bought me something special while we were out shopping. He used to bring me little presents from his business trips when he took them. And he could make me laugh…a lot. He was quiet but he could be very social. We had a couple of backyard parties and he was always the perfect host. I might add…he was one terrific salesman. He could sell anything, Trent. He sold electronics and electronic components and software…things like that. Before that, he sold insurance, and before that, cars...both new and used. He was always the top salesman."

"What did he do for fun?"

"Fun? He loved amusement parks and zoos. Sometimes we would just stay home and watch a good comedy. He loved comedy movies. We would go dancing at times. I enjoyed that more than he did, but he went to make me happy."

"When do you think you could talk to Lindy?"

"I'll try to contact her this afternoon." Trent nodded his approval.

Loraine stepped out into the backyard to water the flowers and pull a few weeds. She quietly hummed to herself as she worked in her efficient manner. As she tidied up the flower bed she thought about Nelson and all she had told Trent. It was all true. Sadly, she realized that Nelson would have been different if he had been a father, and she realized that she was to blame for that not happening. She couldn't have children. That had really affected her because she had desperately wanted a child when she and Nelson were together. He never said anything, but she realized now that he was just as disappointed as she had been. Now there was Trent. It was obvious that Trent needed Nelson, but it was also obvious that Nelson needed Trent, and had needed him for years. Without hesitation, she went inside and picked up the telephone and dialed Lindy's number.

Lindy was at home and seemed glad that Loraine had called, and was even happier when Loraine asked if she could visit. They hadn't seen each other since the week after Nelson went to prison. Loraine was thankful that Lindy didn't hold any of Nelson's crime against her, but today might just be a turning point in their relationship. She couldn't think about those consequences though. She had to think of Trent--this seventeen year old boy who desperately wanted to have his father in his life. Yes, it was a lot to ask of Lindy, but surely she would understand the need to have an attentive father. She sure could have used one when she was seventeen. Loraine sighed as she readied herself to leave for Lindy's.

"Trent, I'm leaving now. You'll be okay?" Loraine called to him from the living room. He opened the bedroom door and quickly appeared.

"Yeah, I'll be okay. My mom should be here soon anyway."

Loraine nodded, and then stepped into the garage. Before she started the car she raised the garage door with her remote, and then waved to Trent as he stood in the doorway watching. She detected his anxiety as the corners of his mouth tipped upward and he halfheartedly waved back. Loraine knew that there was a lot riding on this visit to Lindy, and she hoped that the outcome would be favorable for everybody concerned.

Chapter 33

Lindy smiled widely when she opened the door to Loraine. "It's so good to see you, Loraine. How have you been?"

"I'm fine. You? Ricky? The kids?"

"We're all doing well. Just enjoying the summer before Samantha starts school. First grade! I can't believe it! Come on in and sit down. The kids are in the back yard with my brother. Ricky's at work, so I have some time to just enjoy your company. How about a glass of iced tea?"

"That sounds fine," Loraine smiled and then bit her lip; a habit she had when she was nervous about something. Trent's plea made her nervous. Lindy had been traumatized by Nelson—twice. How would she feel about meeting his son? Nothing was poor Trent's fault, though. He was a victim in all of Nelson's actions, too. She waited as Lindy poured the iced tea into two tall frosted glasses and then joined her at the kitchen table, setting the glasses down in front of each of them.

"So...Loraine.....what's new? Something is going on...I can tell."

"Yes, Lindy....I've had quite a surprise, or should I say shock, this past week."

"What is it?" Lindy was concerned. Was something wrong with Loraine? She waited for Loraine to go on.

"Well...I have a couple of house guests right now. A woman and her son are visiting me from Virginia. The son...is Nelson's son."

Lindy gasped. H-how? When? When did this happen?"

"Apparently when he went looking for you in South Carolina he met her; they had a fling; she got pregnant. Until this week, Nelson had no idea he was a father. The boy is...sixteen or seventeen now and he looks just like Nelson. According to Lois, his mother, he has been tormented all his life about not knowing his father. She brought him to this area to try and find Nelson. Of course, Nelson had given her a fake name so she hadn't had any luck finding him in the past, but she did have my address."

"How much does he know about Nelson?"

"Everything. But the boy is so desperate to have a

father he doesn't care."

"What is the mother like?"

"Sweet….gentle…not a mean bone in her body. Nelson's type."

Lindy nodded as her eyes seemed to go far away for the moment. She was remembering it all, Loraine guessed. This was going to be harder than she thought.

"Anyway, the son wants to meet you."

"Me? Why?"

"He says he wants to try to understand why his father did the things he did."

"Loraine, I couldn't. No. I can't meet him. The memory of all of it is just still too painful. I wouldn't want to take it out on the boy. I mean….I would already be put off by him. It's just too much to expect."

"I guess I know that. I promised the boy that I would ask, but I understand how you feel. It's just that….well, Lindy…the boy is a gentle soul like his mother and very troubled. He's very intelligent and sort of….haunting in a way."

"He's Nelson's son, Loraine. I couldn't possibly meet him."

"Are you talking about John? John has a son?" The sweet voice of Samantha broke into their conversation. Neither Lindy nor Loraine had seen her come in. "Mommy? Does John have a kid?"

"Honey, why don't you take some cookies outside for you, Michael, and Uncle Chris?"

"Can't we meet John's kid? I want to, Mommy! Please? John said he always wanted a kid, and now he has one. Can't we meet him?"

"Because we can't, Sammie. John was mean to us."

"He wasn't mean to me. We had fun. All he wanted was a kid, and now he has one of his own. I want to meet his kid, Mommy!"

Samantha's pleas were interrupted by the front door opening. Ricky walked through the door carrying a briefcase and a bag of treats for after dinner. Samantha skipped to the door blurting out her new information. "Daddy! John has a kid and he wants to meet us. Can we, Daddy? Can we?"

Ricky scooped Samantha up into his arms and kissed her cheek. "What are you babbling about, Princess?" He acknowledged Loraine as he bent to kiss Lindy's cheek. "Loraine, this is a surprise. I wondered who that car belonged to."

"She came to tell us about John's kid, Daddy. He

wants to meet us. Can he? Please? I want to see him."

Ricky put Samantha down. "Go outside and play with Michael, Sweetheart. I want to talk to your mommy." Loraine caught the hardness forming behind the smolder in Ricky's eyes.

"I'm sorry. Samantha wasn't supposed to hear any of that." She apologized.

"What is this about?" Ricky asked, looking from Loraine to Lindy. They filled him in on the subject as his eyes went from dark brown to black. He sipped at the tea Lindy had set in front of him before speaking. "Why does the kid want to meet Lindy?"

"He says he wants to understand his father's obsession with her." Loraine offered.

Ricky reached for Lindy's hand and held onto it. "While my first instinct is to say absolutely not, I have to remember how it was for Lindy. She didn't understand her father's actions for the longest time, and she was very hurt by them." Ricky looked directly at Lindy. "Honey, it's up to you. I feel for the kid, so if you want to meet him, that's fine. If not, that's fine, too. I'm just trying to put myself in this kid's place. After all these years of wanting to know who his father is, he finally finds out. He has to be disappointed, so he's trying to figure out why his dad did the things he did. After all, he has his dad's genes. He may be thinking that he is capable of hurting someone, too."

Lindy was silent as she stared at Ricky and then down at her glass of tea. When she looked up at Ricky and then Loraine, her eyes were shimmering with tears.

"Okay...I'll meet him. I didn't think of it that way."

"Yay! When are we going?" Samantha piped up from behind Ricky.

"Who said you are going anywhere?" Ricky asked his little daughter.

"Because I want to go! John was my friend! It's not his fault I got sick!"

"We'll all go....as a family." Ricky decided. "How will that be?"

"That would be great. How about Saturday? Come for a luncheon cookout. I'll throw some barbequed chicken and a couple of hot dogs on the grill. How is that?"

Loraine left shortly after the arrangements were made. Lindy was unusually quiet as she prepared the evening meal. Ricky busied himself making a salad after he changed out of his work clothes.

"What's wrong, Babe? Are you that apprehensive

about seeing Nelson's son?"

"Well...sorta...but it's more like the anticipation of seeing him. Loraine said he looks like Nelson."

"Oh...she didn't tell me that part. Is this going to be too hard on you?'

"No...yes...I don't know. I keep thinking about what you said....about his wanting to understand his father's actions. You're right. And anyway...it's not the boy's fault. Trent....I like that name. I'm curious about the mother. Loraine said she's a very sweet gentle person."

"Then she would be a lot like the woman I married." Ricky smiled down at Lindy and draped his arm around her shoulders, quickly kissing her forehead.

"I'm doing this for the boy. You know that, don't you, Ricky? Kids' feelings are fragile. I remember all too well."

"I know you are, Babe. I'm proud of you for putting your initial feelings behind the importance of this boy's understanding. Kids should know their parents. Everyone has a right to know both a mother and a father.....no matter who it might be."

"I just keep thinking that if Nelson actually cares about this kid, then his incarceration is more than enough punishment for him."

"Yeah, and way too much punishment for...Trent."

Chapter 34

Saturday came too soon. Lindy, Ricky and the children were in the SUV heading toward Loraine's house. Lindy took a deep breath as Ricky pulled the car into Loraine's driveway. A fleeting memory of the first time she was in a car that pulled into this driveway came back to her. It seemed so long ago, but the memory of those two social workers forcing her out of Uncle Nick's house and into this house was still vivid.

"Is this where John lives?" Samantha chimed from the back seat.

"No...he used to," Lindy answered tightly.

"Are you all right, Babe?" Ricky searched her face worriedly. "Maybe this wasn't such a good idea."

"No....I'll be okay. Just the memories came back suddenly, in Technicolor."

"Are we going in, Daddy?" Samantha's voice reflected her excitement and anticipation of meeting Nelson's son.

Lindy sighed. "Samantha was a victim, too, but she seems able to deal with it. I guess I can, too." Lindy smiled at Ricky and opened her door. As they walked toward the house, she focused on her children. "You two must behave here. Do you understand?"

"Yes," they answered together.

Ricky rang the bell and the door was opened almost immediately. Loraine answered the door smiling at them and ushered them inside. "Would the kids like to go into the back yard? Trent set up a couple of games out there, plus a big exercise ball. Kids seem to like that."

"Where is John's son?" Samantha asked.

"Where is John's son?" Michael parroted.

"He's in the bedroom getting dressed. You'll see him soon." Loraine assured them as she walked toward the sliding doors and opened them.

Samantha and Michael quickened their steps when they saw the yard with the ball and the badminton net set up. Even though they had a yard full of expensive playthings, this seemed to appeal to them because it was different, Lindy guessed. She was sure her offspring would be busily contented for awhile. She looked to her right into the kitchen and spied the woman she knew had to be Lois standing at the sink washing and cutting vegetables. Slowly, Lindy moved toward the kitchen. Lois turned when she felt her presence.

"Well, hello," she welcomed in her soft southern drawl. "You must be Lindy. I'm Lois," she added needlessly.

Lindy liked Lois instantly. She could tell that Lois was kind and gentle, just as Loraine had told her. "So you're from Virginia?" Lindy asked, not knowing what else to say. Lois nodded.

"All my life," she told her, glancing up as Ricky entered the kitchen. "And this is Ricky, your husband? I'm pleased to meet you."

After an awkward silence, Ricky nodded and said, "Same here."

"Can I get you something to drink? Beer? Soda? Iced tea?"

Both Ricky and Lindy chose the iced tea and accepted the glasses from Lois. Loraine came in from the back yard and joined them.

"The kids are having fun with that ball. Hear them laughing?"

Lindy was about to make a comment but when she glanced toward the sliding doors, her eyes landed on a boy of about sixteen or seventeen, leaning against the door frame. He smiled quickly and tentatively at her, but said nothing.

"Lindy and Ricky, this is my son, Trent. Come on in here and say hello, Trent."

Trent couldn't take his eyes off Lindy. "Hi," he said, softly.

"Hi," Lindy repeated, just as softly. Ricky offered his hand, which Trent accepted.

"I'm Ricky DeCelli, and this is my wife, Lindy," he introduced them, although there was no need for it.

"I'm Trent Watkins, Lois and Nelson's son. It's good to meet you."

Nice manners, Lindy acknowledged. Lois must be a good mother. Her thoughts were interrupted by Samantha's sweet voice. "Mommy, Michael has to go pee!" Trent started laughing as Ricky got up and headed toward his young son who was standing there doing the common 'I have to pee' dance. Loraine directed him to the bathroom down the hall. Samantha turned her attention to Trent.

"You're John's son, 'cause you look like him. But you're a *big* kid! I thought you would be little, 'cause

John said he didn't have any kids. Then he had one, and you should be littler than Michael."

Trent looked confused.

"She calls your dad John because he told her that was his name. Samantha, John didn't know he had Trent."

"Why not? How can you not know you have a kid?"

"It's a long complicated story and I'll explain it to you in ten years," Lindy laughed and rolled her eyes. "She's six going on thirty," she informed Trent and Lois.

Trent laughed again. "What is your name?" He asked.

"Samantha Renee DeCelli. My brother is Michael Raymond DeCelli. What is your whole name?"

"Trent Riley Watkins. How old are you, Samantha?"

"Six. I'm six and Michael is four."

"Do you go to school?"

"Yes! I am going to first grade this year! I'm not a baby any more!"

"Wow! You are getting old!"

"How old are you?"

"I'm sixteen."

"That's ten years older than me! Why didn't John know about you?"

"Because I lived in a different state." All four adults approved of his answer, and it seemed to appease Samantha, since the questioning along that line stopped.

"Where is John, anyway?"

"Samantha, that's enough questions for now. Give Trent a break here." Lindy interrupted.

"Samantha, want to go outside and play badminton with me and Michael?" Ricky asked, just knowing that it was the perfect time for Samantha to go so that Trent and Lindy could talk. Samantha agreed to go outside, but looked back at Trent.

"Trent, will you come out and play in a little while?" Trent assured her that he would be out in a little while as Ricky and the children moved through the sliding doors.

The house was suddenly too quiet. Trent looked directly at Lindy and she felt a jolt through her body. Those eyes! They were exactly like Nelson's. He looked like Nelson—except he was shorter and thinner, and of course his hair was longer. Lindy steeled herself, determined not to let the history with Nelson hurt this boy. Loraine had been right—he looked tormented. Lindy knew she had to say something to him, but she felt breathless. She worked at calming herself and then attempted a smile.

"So you wanted to meet me?"

"Yes,"

"Why?"

"I don't know exactly. I think I just wanted to understand."

"And?"

"And I understand why my father was obsessed with you. You're beautiful and you're probably very sweet. A lot like my mom...but why wasn't he obsessed with her?"

"It goes way beyond that, Trent. It was my mother he was obsessed with. I was just a look-alike substitute. He loved my mother since high school but she ran with a different crowd. Her family had money and his family was basically hired hands on a farm. She was way out of his league, he always thought. When I came along, it brought back all those inadequacies he felt years before and was determined to overcome. I know that now and I understand it. It doesn't make it right, but I understand it."

Trent nodded.

"Taking Samantha was a whole other matter. I know it really wasn't his fault that she got the infection that almost killed her, but he shouldn't have taken her. He thought I owed him something for the time he spent in prison. All he wanted was money to get out of the country....I know that. I also know now that he would have never hurt Samantha. I believe that Nelson isn't really a hardened criminal. He's just very misguided. I think his bad childhood did more damage to him than anybody realizes."

Trent sat down as he listened to what Lindy had to say. Even though she was the victim, she wasn't really saying anything bad about his father. That was good, wasn't it?

"Do you hate my dad?"

"I did....but I don't any more. I was young, Trent. I was a few months older than you are right now when I came here to stay. I was terrified of him. Now that I'm older, I know not to fear him. I just hope he is getting help while he's incarcerated."

"If he is getting help, would you agree to a lesser sentence for him? Maybe even parole?"

Lindy was stunned. She did not expect that question. Is this what the meeting was all about? Is this the reason Trent wanted to meet her? To ask her to relent and then go to bat for Nelson? My God! He stole her child! *But he didn't hurt her. This boy needs his father. Remember when you needed yours?* But Nelson committed a felony! *But nobody except Nelson actually got hurt. Remember? Ricky almost killed Nelson.* Lindy swallowed hard.

"Trent, I don't think I have anything to say about that. Nelson committed a felony. I can't change that."

"But you could ask for leniency, couldn't you? His lawyer said you could and it might help. Would you think about it? I know you're a nice person...and that's why I even suggested it. Please....would you just think about it? I really want to know my dad. I just want a father. It's all I ever wanted."

Carole McKee

Chapter 35

Lindy spent the rest of the day in a fog. On one hand, she tried to enjoy the cook-out and the fun her two children seemed to be having, but on the other hand, her mind was reeling, silently repeating Trent's plea to her. Could she actually do that? Could she just say *'okay, he made a mistake, but give Nelson a break?'* NO! She couldn't. He had wronged her and her daughter. It was unforgivable. *Wasn't it?* But Trent is being punished for a crime he didn't commit. *Remember, Lindy? Remember what it was like to have an absentee father?* Having Trent may be the best thing for Nelson, too. He really never had someone he was responsible for.

As she walked onto the patio, she noticed Samantha, still as a statue, perched on a lawn chair. "What are you doing, Sweetheart?"

"Shhh! Trent is drawing my picture," she

whispered.

Lindy crept past Samantha and looked over Trent's shoulder. He was indeed, drawing and creating a close likeness to Samantha. He was a good artist.

"That's really good, Trent. You are very talented."

"My mom says I get it from my dad because she can't even draw stick figures."

"I wasn't aware that Nelson had art talent."

"Yes, he could draw well," Loraine interjected. "Trent, I'll have to show you some of the stuff he drew. There is a drawing of Nelson's hanging on the wall in the den. I thought it was so good I just couldn't part with it when I got rid of all his things."

"I'd like to see some of it," Trent responded.

"Hey, why don't you sit that still for me?" Ricky's voice interrupted the scene.

"Ricky is an artist, Trent. He has done paintings of the kids and it's like drawing action figures most of the time. They don't sit still."

"You're pretty good," Ricky praised as he looked over Trent's shoulder.

"Thanks."

"Where's Michael, Ricky?"

"He's sleeping on the sofa. I carried him in about five minutes ago. He's been hard at play since we got here. We have a yard full of playthings and equipment, but he seemed to have more fun here." Ricky casually draped his arm around Lindy's shoulder.

"That's because it's different than home. I can remember when I was little, my mom would take me to Aunt Jackie's and I would spend hours just playing with her collection of rabbits. She had all kinds of glass figurines of rabbits that she collected and I played with them, even gave them names. I had toys at home, but those rabbits were just new and different." Trent felt his face get hot. He never said so much at one time to a complete stranger, and now he was embarrassed. Ricky picked up on it and decided to put Trent at ease.

"Yeah, you're right. Anything new and different seems more attractive to kids. I was the same way." He smiled at Trent, suddenly liking him very much. He could tell that Lindy liked Trent, and Samantha was enthralled by him. The only DeCelli not captivated by Trent's charm was Michael; but then Michael was Michael—a marcher to his own beat—a beat that nobody else seemed to hear. He was a real character.

Trent tore off the page featuring Samantha's face and handed it to her.

"Are you going to do Michael's now?" She asked.

"Sure. I think I've seen enough of him to do his picture from memory. You really look out for your little brother, don't you?"

"Always," Lindy and Ricky responded in unison.

"I wish I had a brother or sister. It seems kind of nice that way."

"Oh...it has its moments," Lindy laughed.

"Mommy, Trent has a cat named Riley. He's a big gray cat with golden eyes like Trent's. He sleeps on Trent's bed and his Aunt Jackie is watching the cat for him."

Lindy smiled at Trent and then at Samantha. "You two have become friends, haven't you?"

"Yeah, and Trent likes it here. He says we're all nicer than the people in Ginra."

"Virginia, Honey. Trent lives in Virginia."

"Is that like Narnia?"

Trent burst out laughing. "Something like Narnia," he joked.

"Mommy, can Trent come to our house?"

"Not tonight, but he can come over sometime if he wants."

"Thank you, Lindy. I would like that. My mother, too?"

"Of course, Trent. You're both welcome."

When Trent finished his drawing of Michael, the DeCelli family prepared to leave. Lindy and Ricky thanked Loraine for a lovely day and promised to keep in touch. Samantha reminded them that they said Trent could come to their house, and they reiterated that he could come over sometime. The drive home was relatively quiet.

Lindy and Ricky quickly bathed the children and tucked them in and met each in the kitchen for a cup of herbal tea, a practice they had been doing for years. Ricky already had the kettle on the burner. Lindy retrieved the cups from the cabinet and set them on the counter, while Ricky got out the teabags, sugar and cream for Lindy's tea. They didn't speak until they were sitting at the table with a cup of tea in front of them.

"So are you going to tell me what you and Trent talked about?"

"Oh....yeah....Ricky, I don't know what he thinks I can do...but he wants me to go to bat for Nelson."

"How? What does he think you should do?"

"I'm not sure, exactly. I'm not sure I even *could* do something to help him. I don't know, Ricky. I can't see myself doing anything good for Nelson, but on the other hand, that boy's sad eyes are haunting me. Lois told me that he was always hoping his father would show up the whole time he was growing up. He started getting into trouble when he realized that wasn't going to happen. What do you think I should do, Ricky?"

"I have no idea, Babe."

"But you have a stake in this, too. Sammie is your daughter, too. How do you feel about Nelson getting a break for taking your—our daughter?"

"Well, of course I don't like that idea, but Trent's eyes are haunting me, too. Somehow it suddenly is not about Nelson any more."

"I know. I want to ease that boy's anxiety, but the only way to do it is to do something positive for Nelson. But maybe that's what it's all about."

Ricky jerked his head up suddenly and stared at Lindy. "What do you mean?"

"Maybe by doing something positive....doing something good for Nelson, I will be able to get over my animosity towards him. Maybe helping him would set me free of the torment I go through every time I think of those things he did."

"If that's how you feel, Babe, maybe you should consider helping Trent."

"I think I will call his lawyer on Monday and see what he says." Lindy stood up and slid onto Ricky's lap, draping an arm around his neck. Ricky pulled her close and kissed her cheek.

"You know that no matter what you decide, I'll stand by you, don't you?" He searched her face for tell-tale signs of indecisiveness.

Lindy smiled at him. "I never doubted that for a second."

Carole McKee

Chapter 36

Lindy rose from the comfortable wingchair when the door to the attorney's office opened. The attorney spotted her instantly. He smiled as he extended his hand and introduced himself.

"Thank you so much for coming in, Mrs. DeCelli. I was a little surprised by your call...but I take it you have met Trent."

"Yes, I have. Nice kid."

"Yes, he is. So what are you here to talk about?"

Lindy pulled in a deep breath and slowly let it out. This was still going to be very difficult. Now she wished she had taken Ricky up on his offer to come with her. As she slid into the chair in front of the attorney's desk, she felt her resolve returning.

"Attorney Bingham, I understand that you told

Trent that I could do something to lessen Nelson's sentence. I don't quite understand what you are talking about. How can I do anything? He committed a felony. I can't go back and say it was all a misunderstanding...that I forgot he was babysitting that day."

"No, of course not....but if you are willing to forgive him then he could be put on the eligibility list for parole. Right now there is no forgiveness for him at all. With your forgiveness and my plea for Trent's needs I could get something worked out in order for Trent and Nelson to get to spend some quality time together."

Lindy rose from the chair, walked to the window, and stared outside unseeingly and silently. Bingham stared after her, just knowing that her mind was in turmoil. He was giving her the distance she needed as he quietly waited. Finally, Lindy turned from the window, returned to her seat in front of Dave Bingham's desk, and broke the silence.

"Attorney Bingham...Nelson Sutter is a felon. First, he raped me and then he kidnapped my daughter. How can anyone expect me to just pardon him for that? Yes, I want to do something to help Trent. I see the pain in his eyes. I see it, and I know what it feels like to have an absentee father. But yet...I can't ignore the crimes either."

"Mrs. DeCelli...he paid for what he did to you,

personally. Now he's paying for what he did to your daughter. Keep in mind that he didn't hurt her."

"I know he didn't hurt her. As a matter of fact...Samantha likes him. She even includes him in her prayers at night." Lindy made a sound that came close to a tiny laugh.

"You know....even if you're willing to forgive him there are no guarantees that anything will come of it. Federal crimes are not just dismissible. The things Nelson did and his reasons for doing them were incredibly stupid....I admit. I've known Nelson for years. He's a little mixed up at times, but he is no hardened criminal."

"Coulda' fooled me," Lindy shot back, causing him to inwardly flinch. Lindy's eyes went to the window again while the attorney quietly watched her. He could only imagine how hard this was for her. It must have taken a lot of courage to come in to talk to him about Nelson, and for that he admired her. "Look...Attorney Bingham...."

"Dave....please call me Dave."

"All right...Dave...let me think about this for a couple of days. Let me do some research into the system. I'd like to get my husband's input...although he says the decision is mine and he'll stand by whatever I decide. But Samantha is his daughter, too...so I want his thoughts on this."

"Mrs. DeCelli...that's all I can ask of you. Will you be in touch?"

"Yes....and please call me Lindy." She stood up and extended her hand to him. After a brief handshake Lindy walked out of the office. Dave watched her go, knowing in his heart that whatever she came up with would be fair.

The ride home was short but the distraction was long and far. What should she do? She loathed Nelson but she liked Trent. Who should win out here? It can only be one way: win, win and lose, lose. Those were the options. She hoped Ricky would be able to provide her with some of his inner wisdom. In the meantime, she would research all options concerning prison release and early releases, and pardons; and do a little soul searching as well.

Diane, her father's wife greeted her when she walked into her house. "Fresh coffee, Lindy. I just made it."

"Good....I could use a cup and I could use some words of wisdom right now. So I'd like to hear your opinion on this....whatever this is. Save Trent or pardon Nelson—depending on how you look at it."

"Well, we can talk about it if you want to. Your dad

took the kids to McDonald's for lunch."

"Those two are going to look like Happy Meals," Lindy protested. "Sorry…I'm just on edge. I am happy that he enjoys spoiling them like he does."

"Well, you have a big weight on your shoulders right now, Lindy."

"Yeah….a teenaged boy's happiness is dependent on me. I get to decide if this kid has a father or not. Crazy, isn't it?"

"Yes, it is. But, Lindy…I know…that between your head and your heart, you'll come up with a decision that is wise and kind at the same time. Because that's who you are."

Long after her father and Diane left, Lindy mulled over the circumstances surrounding Nelson and Trent. She wanted to do the right thing, but what was the right thing? Actions have consequences and Nelson should have to suffer the consequences. But should Trent have to? If Nelson's consequences ended, would she then begin to suffer?

Suddenly it came to her. Lindy knew what she had to do, and it would be the hardest thing she ever did. She had to face Nelson. She had to see him, be in the same room with him, and talk to him, before she could make any decisions. Swallowing hard, she made up her mind that she would confront, head on, the monster that had caused her nightmares over the past fifteen years.

Chapter 37

Lindy and Nelson's attorney sat in silence inside the attorney-prisoner visiting room. Lindy's brain was racing a mile a minute, yet there was not one definable thought. All of her nerve endings stood at attention, just waiting for the monster to enter the room. She forced her clenched fists to relax and open when she realized that her nails were digging into the palms of her hands.

Maybe this is all wrong. Maybe I shouldn't be here. Her head spoke in volumes but her heart remained silent. Suddenly, the jingle of keys interrupted her thoughts and she braced herself as the door swung open.

And there he was, standing there, looking puzzled. Lindy stared at Nelson, wondering when he had gotten smaller and....older. She saw the shock register on his face when he recognized her.

"Lindy," he said, as he stood there with his feet

glued to the cement floor under him. His throat constricted and it felt like there was a giant hairball stuck in it.

"Nelson, sit down. We only have an hour, tops." Dave protested.

Nelson silently ordered his feet to move toward the table and then he slid onto the chair across from Lindy. He couldn't take his eyes off of her, but this time it wasn't because of lust. It was fear—an indefinable fear that he couldn't quite understand. He had harmed this girl-woman once. He had overpowered her, and yet he was terrified of her now. She focused her eyes and looked directly into his eyes, and he flinched, diverting his eyes to the table.

"Are you surprised to see me, Nelson?" She asked, needlessly.

"Yeah," he almost whispered, but nodded his head.

"I've met Trent. He's a nice kid, but I guess his mother gets all the credit for that."

"Yes, he is….and yes, she deserves all the credit for that. I only wish I'd have known about him." Lindy could hear the regret in his voice.

"Things sometimes happen for a reason, Nelson…and consequences must be served."

"You're right. I guess this is my punishment for

taking your daughter. How is Samantha, by the way?"

"She's fine, but she is not the topic of conversation here."

"I know. And now I know how you must have felt when I took her, because I know how I feel that I can't be with my son. It's funny, but....I remember thinking about how Samantha would feel when she realized she wasn't going to see her parents any more. I almost changed my plans then. I wanted to hurt you, but I never wanted to hurt Samantha."

"Why did you want to hurt me, Nelson?"

"I don't know, Lindy. I was all mixed up back then. I guess you know that I spent most of my life being in love with your mother...but of course, I didn't have any idea that it was your mother. I knew I was never good enough for Stacey...but I loved her with all my heart for years. When I saw you...her look-alike...it almost made me angry. I felt as though ....I don't know exactly....like God was screwing with me, I guess. Putting the two of you in my path...and I couldn't have either one of you. I don't know how else to say it. It drove me crazy." Lindy just nodded while her eyes remained riveted to his.

"I'm sorry, Lindy. From the bottom of my heart, I am sorry for what I've done to you. I mean that."

"I believe you," she answered.

"You do?"

"Yes, Nelson...I do. But I don't know what everybody expects me to do for you. A felony is a felony. My feelings aren't going to change that."

"I know. I'm satisfied that you believe I'm sorry."

"Nelson...I forgive you. But my forgiving you might not be what it takes to help your son."

"I know. I realize that. I screwed up...big time. You know...he's been here three times and already that's all I look forward to...is his visits. You said that you forgive me. Do you? Really?"

"Yes...Really. I forgive you. I never realized just how screwed up you were. I always thought of you as some sort of monster. I never saw you for what you were...injured. You were an emotionally injured person all of you life. I get that now. I can look at you through clinical eyes now. You told my daughter that you always wanted a kid, didn't you?"

"Yeah...I guess I did. Samantha and I had some great talks. She's a brilliant child."

"Yes...she is. And for some reason, she seems to like you." Lindy responded with a smile—her first smile since she'd been in the room. "Ricky and I have been blessed with two beautiful, intelligent children."

"Well...they take after their parents. I can see

that."

"You, however...have been blessed with a son—a talented one. You've lost so much time with him already." Lindy stood up as she heard the jingling of the keys outside the door. "I'll see what I can do, Nelson. That's all I can say."

As the door swung open, Nelson turned toward it, but then turned back to Lindy. "Thank you Lindy. I mean that."

As he started through the door, flanked by the guards, Lindy glimpsed the tears in the corners of his eyes.

Chapter 38

The drive home was silent. As soon as Nelson's attorney dropped Lindy off, she went straight to the computer to do some research on penal punishment options. Samantha and Michael were with her brother Chris and his wife Cindy for a day at the zoo, so Lindy knew she had the rest of the afternoon. When the telephone rang, she answered it at the computer desk.

"Hi, Babe….how did it go?" Ricky's welcome voice came over the line.

"It…it went okay. Nelson didn't appear as ominous to me as he once did. Actually, Ricky…he's not all that big…and he's really getting old. He's sad. I could see it in his eyes. He's sad and sorry. Ricky….I….I forgive him."

"Enough to agree to his getting out of prison?"

"If I had that much power….yes. But I don't have that kind of authority or power. I'm researching alternatives to maximum security prisons now. What do you think?"

"I think I love my sweet, adorable wife. Honey, if you want I'll help you look into it. You know...forgiving Nelson will help you heal."

"It already has, Sweetheart. All the hate and malice I felt for Nelson is gone. I just want his son to benefit from finding his father."

"I love you. I'll be home early today so we can look into it together."

Lindy decided to put the research aside and wait for Ricky, since he was so much better at research than she was. She took advantage of the kids' absence by cleaning the house and then she popped a cake in the oven. Lindy was frosting the cake with white frothy frosting, hiding the cut up strawberry torte mixture in between the layers, when Ricky walked in the door. He watched as she used a few cut up strawberries to decorate the top of the cake.

"That's beautiful," he complimented. "Am I cooking on the grill tonight? I guess Chris and Cindy will be here for dinner, right?"

"I think so. I have potato salad and there's corn. I'll make a lettuce salad and we can eat on the patio."

Knowing they had at least another hour before

everyone got there, they both went to the computer. Lindy covered the cake before they went to the computer, to keep Butter, their yellow Labrador retriever from being tempted to reach up and help himself. Ricky sat in front of the monitor and Lindy pulled up a chair beside him. Together they began researching options to make Nelson more available to his son.

***

Long after Chris and Cindy left, and the children were in bed, they sat at the computer scouring website after website, delving into penal laws, and looking for exceptions to the law.

Sighing, Lindy leaned back into her chair and stared at Ricky. "Maybe we should just see what his attorney can do for him. If the attorney can get something going, and I approve it.....maybe that's all I have to do."

"Maybe you're right. We're not lawyers or judges. We really don't know what can be accomplished."

"I'll call the attorney in the morning. Right now, I'm ready for bed."

"Me, too," Ricky responded, as he began shutting down the computer.

Lindy slept fitfully for the first time in years, and when she awoke in the morning, she felt a sense of freedom descend upon her. She was free—free from the hate, the fear, and the vengeance she harbored over the past sixteen years. The time had come to brighten the future of one sixteen-year-old boy and let the past fall into the shadows. She knew what she had to do, and she planned on starting her mission right after her family ate breakfast.

All of the research Lindy and Ricky had done helped to formulate the plan in which Lindy would follow. Her plan had only been tried twice--with positive results--in entire the state, and she would see to it that it was attempted a third time. The positive results were up to Nelson.

Chapter 39

"Dad! Hi!" Nelson stood up among the rows of planted beets and waved at his son as he stood outside the fence. "I'm coming in to help...okay?"

"Okay! See ya in a few!" Nelson responded with a grin.

It had been two months since he had been moved to this farming facility, and he couldn't be happier. There were only three such containment facilities in the country: one in Pennsylvania, one in California, and one in Arkansas. Unluckily there were none in the state of Virginia, where Lois and Trent were from.

These facilities were minimum security, and family was encouraged to visit. The fifteen-hundred acre farm grew crops and raised animals, all maintained by non-violent inmates who were chosen by high-ranking officials. The products from the farm were sold at a local market, and the money earned, along with a small government subsidy, made the farm a profitable venture. Nelson had no idea how Lindy pulled it off, but she got him in there by the approval of the State Governor. She had been by once to see him since he'd been there. She had pointed out how ironic it was that he ended up back on a farm. He had replied by telling her that he was still afraid of the rooster. When it was his turn to feed the chickens he gave the big rooster a wide berth.

Although the farm had no containment fences, no prisoner left the property. Each was required to wear an ankle bracelet that set off a blaring alarm if anyone should step over the boundaries of the farm. Nelson knew it would be stupid to do that because it automatically meant being returned to a lock-up. The inmates slept in buildings similar to bunk houses on a ranch, four to a room. The three buildings each had five sleeping rooms, a small kitchen, with a large dining room off of it, and a sitting room that held chairs, two sofas and a television. There was a small recreation room off of the sitting room where inmates could play table tennis or sit at a table and play cards. A large dorm-type bathroom held five shower stalls, four enclosed toilets, and four sinks. All of the inmates got along, and there was never any reason to fear any one of them, since they were all non-violent captives.

Once a month each inmate was allowed a weekend outside the facility. Nelson loved those weekends. Since Lois had found him, she had left the state of Virginia and moved to a small town near the farm. She quickly got a job at a small insurance company and found a place to rent. On his weekends, Lois picked him up and they went to her rental. Usually they just stayed at home but occasionally Nelson treated them to dinner with his meager earnings on the farm.

Lois seemed to enjoy his visits, but it was Trent who flourished from them. He and Nelson tossed a ball back and forth in their small yard, or played with the X-Box. When Trent had weekend homework, Nelson helped him with it. Trent was filling out a little and was now just about the same height as Nelson. There was no doubting that they were father and son, since they looked so much alike. Lois noticed that since he was spending a lot of time outdoors, Nelson was regaining his healthy look and was once again the attractive man he had been years ago. And they were getting close. Lois wondered where it was going to lead as she sat in the car waiting for Trent and Nelson to come out of the front entrance for his weekend off. She couldn't help but smile when she saw them coming, side by side, laughing and talking. They even walked alike, she realized.

"You're looking beautiful as ever, Lois," Nelson said, as he entered the car.

"Yeah, right, Nelson….in my old faded jeans and tank top," she countered.

"It's not what you wear, Lois...it how you wear it," he responded. "How about a picnic this weekend? Maybe do some swimming. What do ya think?"

"Sounds good. What do you think, Trent?" She turned toward the back seat.

"Yeah...that's a great idea. A lot of my new friends will be at the lake. Can we go there?"

"Yep, sounds like a fine idea to me." Nelson agreed. "So how's everything, Lois? Job okay? Any problems you want to talk about?"

"No....everything is fine. I love my job, the bills are paid, and that little bit you send helps me a lot. Of course the money Trent gets from the state helps."

"Yeah, that's actually part of my pay. I'm glad that after all this time I can finally say I'm contributing to my son's needs."

"You are, Nelson. In more ways than you know." Lois looked over at him and smiled.

"It's good to see that beautiful smile again. Let's stop for breakfast. I'm starving."

The weekend was wonderful for all three of them. Trent was happy to introduce his dad to some of his friends when they were at the lake. He seemed proud of Nelson, or was it that he was just proud to have a dad? It didn't matter either way, because whatever the case, Trent was the better for it.

On Saturday night, long after Trent had turned in for the night, Lois and Nelson sat in her small living room, watching a movie.

"Lois...can I ask you something?" Nelson ventured.

"Of course," she responded.

"Why did you never marry?"

Lois shrugged. "I don't know. I never found anybody."

"But as pretty as you are, you would think somebody would have found you."

"That's sweet, Nelson...thanks. But it just never happened. There was one guy but...." Lois gave Nelson the abbreviated version of her romance with Garrett.

Suddenly, Nelson knew what he wanted. Not only did he want to be a father to Trent, but he wanted to be a husband to Lois. Would she go for it? His thoughts were interrupted when he realized Lois was speaking again.

"Trent has always been my top priority, Nelson. I was very careful concerning who I let come into my life.

Not only did a man have to have total acceptance of Trent but Trent had to have total acceptance of the man. I didn't always find that. Garrett and Trent accepted each other, so that relationship worked, until Garrett's wife showed up. When one of the security officers from Trent's school started hitting on me, I felt Trent's back bristle. And besides, he wasn't all that interested in Trent's welfare."

Nelson nodded, as though he understood. "I truly regret that I didn't go back to Virginia, Lois. When I finally got your letters it was years later. I just assumed that you were married by then and I always wished you well. I never even dreamed we had a son together...or I would have been there in a flash."

They both let the subject drop and Lois went into her room to sleep for the night. Nelson bunked on the sofa. After dinner the next day he would return to the farming facility and have plenty of time to think and plan before his next month's visit.

Chapter 40

The month dragged by. Nelson had rehearsed over and over again what he was going to say to Lois, and in spite of the nagging doubts, he knew he had to propose. What nagged Nelson the most was that it wasn't fair to Lois to put her on the spot like that. She was still young enough and certainly attractive enough to find a man who was not kept behind a fence for around 27 to 28 days a month. But where were her prospects? She moved from the beautiful city of Richmond to this little town near the farming facility. Sure, it was great for Trent, but was it all that great for her? The only single man in the town was around ninety and toothless. It was a small family community.

Nelson's thoughts were interrupted by Trent's shout. "C'mon, Dad! Are you ready? Mom's got the grill all set up."

Nelson grinned at his boy and grabbed his

overnight bag and stood in line to be checked out. It was now or never. Lois sat behind the wheel and waited for Nelson and Trent to join her in the car. She was smiling as she thought about the miraculous change in Trent. He was happy. There had been no trouble since they moved here to this old farming town, and the sweet boy she always knew she had, was back.

Although the pay was not as good as in Virginia, the job was a lot less stress. Even with less pay, she was managing to keep everything paid and even have a little extra, since the cost of living in this town was a lot lower than where they came from. The people she worked with were nice and pleasant, and she was making friends. She missed Jackie, though. Jackie had promised to visit at the end of summer and Lois was looking forward to it. Trent was, too. And he already had plans of introducing Jackie to his father, which was something that seemed to be important to him.

Trent was making friends, too. These farm kids were wholesome and trustworthy, open and friendly. Trent no longer felt as though he had to prove anything to be accepted. He had good friends, and he had what other kids had—a father.

The ride home was pleasant. Trent and Nelson chatted about baseball, with Trent including Lois in on the conversation. Since Lois knew a little about the game, she didn't feel left out and was able to join in with opinions and observations.

After a dinner of grilled fish, asparagus, and potato salad, Lois brought out the lemon cake she had made the night before. It was half devoured in short order, and while Lois cleaned up, Nelson and Trent tossed a baseball back and forth. A pleasant evening came to a close around ten, when Trent turned in for the night.

This was it. Trent was sleeping and he and Lois were in the living room watching television. Nelson cleared his throat and began.

"Lois...remember what I asked you last time I was here?"

"I'm not sure, Nelson.....what?"

"I asked you why you never got married."

"Oh....yeah...you did ask that...didn't you?"

"Lois....I'm just going to ask. Would you consider marrying me?"

"Oh...Nelson....I...are you serious?"

"Yes...serious as a heart attack."

"Why? I mean....why would you want to marry me?"

Nelson thought about it before he spoke. "Because…if I had been in my right mind years ago…I would have gone to Richmond and married you. I didn't get the chance to make it right then, but now I can do the right thing….if you want me. I mean….I'm no prize. I'm a convict, I have nothing, and I'll be that way a long time. I know you can do better, but for some strange reason, you haven't." Nelson stared at Lois for a moment before he continued. "To be honest, Lois….I am in love with you. You can take some time to think about it. I know it's a major decision."

"Yes."

"What?"

"Yes….I'll marry you. But it will have to wait until Jackie gets here around Labor Day. I want her to be my maid of honor."

"Yes, dear…whenever you say….whatever you say." Nelson smiled a genuine smile. "I can't promise you anything, except to love you and our son with all my heart."

"We'll be a family then, Nelson."

"That's right…a true family. Husband, wife, and son."

In the bedroom two rooms away all that could be heard was the quietly whispered word, "Yes."

Trent's world was complete.

The End

Dear Readers;

This completes the "Choices" series. I hope you enjoyed the characters and their stories as much as I did when I created them. Choices bring consequences. In the beginning, choices were made--some good and some not so good. Then the consequences began-- some good and some not. The series ends with consequences being righted by good choices. We have come full circle.

Best regards;

Carole McKee

P.S. Be sure to check out my eBooks at www.Amazon.com

"Kisses from the heart"

"Maddie's Garden"

"Second Chances"

"Going Home"

Carole McKee

22593539R00154